U0094078

哈福

哈福

Good English in 5 min.

5分鐘
征服英語會話

張瑪麗
Scott William◎合著

5分鐘征服，不是奇蹟!
7個方法，讓您大膽開口說

5 分鐘征服，不是奇蹟！

絕大多數的人即使學了一、二十年的英語，碰到老外，仍然是開不了口。這不是危言聳聽，是千真萬確的事實。為什麼會這麼糟糕？

仔細追究原因，不外乎下列幾個因素：

1. 學英語，沒有持之以恆。
2. 沒找到好的方法和教材。
3. 膽子小，害怕開口說英語。
4. 缺乏英語環境，以致於沒有機會練習。

不管是什麼原因，都沒有關係，本書將徹底醫好這些毛病，讓大家即使碰到老外，也敢大膽地說英語！只要按照本書所列的方法和秘訣，5 分鐘征服英語會話，不是奇蹟！

此外，書中也清楚地剖析學不好英語的原因，同時，更提供了七個學好英語的方法，像是：

1. 快速學好發音的方法
2. 快速增加單字量的方法
3. 快速精通文法的方法
4. 快速開口說英語的方法
5. 快速提高聽力的方法
6. 快速提高閱讀能力的方法
7. 快速提高寫作能力的方法

這些問題，書中都有詳細的解答和分析，讓所有人在最短的時間內，可以很快地、輕鬆地把英語學好，用英語和老外聊不停。

本書內容共分三大部份：

Part 1 是英語實力強化篇：教您快速學好英語的七個方法。

Part 2 是輕鬆打開英語話匣子：收集的是平常最實用、最簡單的生活會話，教您快速用英語和老外打開話匣子。

Part 3 是放膽開口說英語：收集的是一般社交應酬場合的英語會話，教您見到老外，可以侃侃而談。

我們的規劃是：

Step 1 要先了解學好英語的七種方法，讓您快速進入英語殿堂。

Step 2 進入簡單會話篇，這時要學的是各種場合的會話，一看就懂、一學就會，可用「直覺就可學會」來形容。

Step 3 是實戰會話篇，這時候，就是展現功夫的時機，一定要把前面所學的實際應用出來，讓老外對你刮目相看！

善用本書，你的英語會話能力，一定高人一等！

在此順祝您

學習成功愉快！

CONTENTS

Chapter 3 交際應酬

Part 3 英語會話的第二步

Chapter 4 社交英語

Chapter 5 寒暄打招呼

Chapter 6 與老外聊天

Part 1
為什麼碰到老外，不敢開口？

Chapter 1　7 個方法，讓您大膽開口說

英語學不好？！

「怎樣把英語學好？」

「學英語有什麼捷徑嗎？」

相信這些都是有心學好英語者最關心的問題。

那麼，到底應該怎麼樣才能把英語學好呢？在這裡，先讓我們來分析一下英語學不好的原因。

一、被天生的惰性擊垮　學英語並不困難，很多人都知道英語的重要性，也很有興趣去學，可是常常在發誓要學好英語的下一刻鐘，就變卦了，雄心壯志沒有了，當初的誓言全忘了。說穿了，就是懶惰在作祟。

二、找不到方法　凡事都必須在立志後，找出方法及目標，腳踏實地去做才能成功。可是，很多學英語的人找不到好方法，學英語就變成一件苦差事，再加學英語的環境不良，鬥志很快就沒有了，心裡很快就萌生「以後再說」的念頭。

三、懼怕　這句英語怎麼說？那句英語怎麼說？想來想去，最後一句都說不出來，就覺得英語很困難了。

事實上，學英語比學中文要容易多了，之所以會害怕，是因為自己欠缺信心和恆心。看看那些英文不錯的人，大部

份都是比較有自信的人。就拿貿易公司的業務員來說吧，他們在和老外應對時，英文說得呱呱叫，但是他們的英語真的就說得很好、很得體嗎？不見得！只是因為他們「不怕」，所以可以輕鬆地和對方溝通。

記得，千萬不要怕，只要能克服恐懼，就能一舉提昇你的英文實力。

在分析了英語學不好的三個原因之後，再來談談要如何學好英語。

學好英語的方法

其實，要徹底把英語學好，達到聽說讀寫皆流利的地步，只有一個辦法，就是去親近「她」！英語是一個值得追求的情人，只要你肯努力追求，總有一天，會得到她的回眸一笑。

不要忘記，英語學不好，百分之九十九點九的責任在於自己；英語學不好，「敵人」不是別人，是自己！

首先，學好英語最重要的，就是打好基礎，這也是初學英語最基本的要求。

如何才能打好英語的基礎呢？在這裡，我們把它歸納成三個重點：**1. 把發音學好；2. 把單字學好；3. 把文法學好。**

現在，就讓我們逐項來為您解說：

如何把發音學好

想學好英語，要先學好發音。

很多人學不好英語，最重要的原因之一，就是忽視了發音的重要性。他們認為，英語最重要的是形和義，因此在不知不覺之間，就違反了學英語的基本規則，進而影響單字的記憶和累積。

不學好發音，自然就沒有辦法拼出正確的單字。因此，碰到不認識的單字，即使努力查字典，也沒辦法讀出準確的音來。這樣一來，久而久之，就會有一種跟不上的無力感。

學發音，一定要知道發音常識，弄清楚發音的部位和方法。至於要怎麼做？最主要當然是，靠口頭模仿和開口練習。

如果是初學者，上課時就必須認真聽課，模仿老師的口型，跟著老師念。下課後，最好透過看網路、YouTube 或聽有聲教材，反覆模仿、練習，才能從和模仿中，體會英語發音的奧妙。

在這裡，我們還要建議您，每天抽出 30 分鐘到 1 小時來大聲朗讀。

朗讀時，時間不要太長。而且一定要持之以恆，不可以一曝十寒或三天打魚兩天曬網，這樣是學不好英語的。

有很多學英語的人，心血來潮一高興，就連續練兩、三個小時，唸到口乾舌燥；高興的時候，連碰也不碰，其實這樣效果並不好。

唸英語時，一定要唸出聲音，這樣才能辨別是不是唸對了，如果錯了，還可以及時糾正。千萬不要怕唸錯了，惹人笑話，最好還要主動爭取老師和同學們的指正，及早糾正錯誤的發音，因為如果成了習慣，就不容易改過來了。

發音學得好不好，關係到單字記不記得住、及聽、說、讀、寫各種能力，是否能順利發展。也就是說，關係到是不是能夠把英語學好。所以，豈可不戒慎哉？

如何把單字學好

說完學發音的方法之後，接下來要談的是學好單字的方法。

「背單字有竅門嗎？」

常有學生這樣問。如果你認為學英語只是記單字，就大錯特錯了。

事實上，單字只是英語的材料之一。好比蓋房子，除了材料，還要有建築方面的技術和本領；學英語也是一樣，要有組字成句的能力才行，如果不了解這一點，就沒辦法學好英語了。

一般說來，大部份的英語單字都有很多意思，如果只是一個字一個字分開來記，不知道每個英語單字之間的關係，是沒有多大用處的。

就拿quarter這個英文字來說吧，quarter這個英語單字，平常用得最多的意思，是四分之一、二角五分硬幣和一刻鐘。

但是，你知道嗎？它也有一季、來源、弦、船尾和饒恕的意思，如果只是一個單字一個單字地記，就無法確切地掌握 quarter 在每一句英語中的意思了。

以下是 quarter 的各種意思

a. 表四分之一

✿ **a quarter of mile**

（四分之一哩）

✿ **not a quarter as good**

（比…差得遠）

b. 表一刻鐘

✿ **The trains come on the quarter.**

（電車每十五分鐘來一班。）

✿ **It's a quarter past 12.**

（現在是十二點十五分。）

c. 表一季，三個月

✿ **They pay my rent by the quarter.**

（他們每三個月付一次租金。）

d. 表來自、來源

✿ **Men running from all quarters.**

（從四面八方跑來的人）

e. 表弦

✿ **the moon at the first quarter**

（上弦月）

✿ **the moon in its last quarter**

（下弦月）

f. 表饒恕

✿ **give quarter**

（給予饒恕）

g. 表船尾

✿ **on the port quarter**

（船尾）

h. 表崗位

✿ **Officers and men once took up their quarters.**

（官兵立即各就各位。）

可見，記單字不能脫離實際的語言來死記硬背，必須結合文章裡的片語和句子一起記。

只記單字，而不管它在語言中的用法，看來省事，實際誤事，很多人在使用英語時，很多的毛病和錯誤就出在這裡。

如果只有死記單字，不但記不牢，而且容易忘記，又費事，又枯燥乏味，連帶地也會影響學習的情緒和效率。

學好單字的主要方法是朗讀、應用和默寫。但是，切勿只死記硬背。一定要透過背誦、默寫課文或句子等途徑，記住單字的形、聲、義，並掌握它的基本用法，才能記得牢。

一曝十寒的方式，是學不好英語的，就算當時能勉強記住，幾天之後又會忘得一乾二淨。記單字可以和發音同時進行，每天朗誦課文，既可以練習發音，又可以記憶和鞏固已學的單字。

在知道如何記單字之後，接下來要學的，就是如何擴大字彙的量。

英語到底有多少單字，沒有人知道，加上我們的時間有限，不可能記下所有的單字，所以只能選擇性地記該記的字。

至於哪些是應該記的單字呢？當然就是最常用的單字了。

一般說來，我們日常生活中最常用的單字，大約是5000字左右，這些單字約佔報章雜誌書籍的99%。亦即，讀100個英語單字，只會遇到一個生字。像這些常用的英語單字，就應該記住它。

常用的英語單字，因為出現頻率高，所以容易記住。如果是一個非常冷僻，而且使用頻率很低的單字，即使下功夫去記，也可能因為很長時間沒再出現，很快就被遺忘了。

對這類單字，我們的建議是，記得住就記，記不住就算了，不要強求。

那麼，到底要記多少單字才夠用？根據語言學家的說法，國中生是 3000 個單字；高中生是 5000 個單字，大學生是 8000 至 10000 個單字，至於研究所的學生就要多達 12000 字了。

這樣的單字數量不算少，萬一沒有記到上述要求的標準時，也不必緊張，因為 L. P. Ayres 博士曾針對歐美人士的英語會話做分析，得出以下這個讓人不可思議的結果：

（1）10 個字中有一個是 the、and。

（2）5 個字中有一個是 of、to、I。

（3）4 個字中有一個是 the、and、of、to、I、a、in、that、you。

所以，在日常英語會話中有 60%，幾乎只用 100 個單字就 OK 了。

可是，很多不知道這個訣竅的人，在學英語時，卻花很多心力去學一些複雜且少用的單字，如：January、February、November、December……。相反地，對於如：a、an、in、of、the、take、get、make……等等，簡單而且常用的單字，反而忽略了。

初學者往往認為這些單字太簡單了，不必下很大功夫去學，但這是錯誤的。這也就是為什麼他們說和寫的能力無法提高，表達能力差的癥結所在。

其實像 January、February、November、December…這些單字很少用，不必花很大力量去學，記得住就記，記不住就算了。而像 a、an、in、of、the、get、make、take 等單字，就要多花一些工夫去學，因為它們雖然拼寫簡單，意義卻千變萬化，往往英語能力的高低，就在這裡分出高下。

記單字有什麼妙招嗎？有以下四種方法：**1. 分類記憶法，2. 視覺記憶法，3. 首尾聯想記憶法，4. 慣用語記憶法**，讓你可以快速又有趣地把單字記起來。

1. 分類記憶法

所謂分類記憶法，就是把日常英語會話中最常用的名詞、形容詞和動詞，用有系統的方式分類整理。

中文的職業有很多，在英語中也有很多有關「職業」的用語，如 poet、nurse、soldier、career、teacher 等等。如果能用聯想的方式去記憶，一會兒功夫，就可以記住很多的單字了。

例如：

a. 有關動物的用語

animal
（動物）

sheep
（羊）

pig
（豬）

tiger
（獅子）

deer
（鹿）

elephant
（象）

b. 有關植物的用語

plant
（植物）

fruit
（水果）

flower
（花）

tree
（樹木）

grass
（草）

rose
（玫瑰）

c. 有關職業的用語

actor
（演員）

housewife
（家庭主婦）

banker
（銀行家）

nurse
（護士）

singer
（歌手）

writer
（作家）

d. 有關家庭的用語

father	son
（父親）	（兒子）
mother	daughter
（母親）	（女兒）
husband	wife
（丈夫）	（妻子）

e. 有關交通的用語

airport	train
（飛機場）	（火車）
ship	traffic
（船）	（交通）
station	ticket
（車站）	（車票）

2. 視覺記憶法

所謂視覺記憶法，顧名思義，就是用眼睛看，然後再去聯想它對應的單字，有點像我們平常說的「看圖說單字」。

就拿客廳的擺設來說吧！你可以想中文的桌子，英文就是 table；中文的花瓶，英文就是 vase；中文的沙發，英文就是 sofa；電視是 television；收音機是 radio；時鐘是 clock；地毯是 carpet；天花板是 ceiling。

像這樣，你是不是很快可以聯想出很多有關客廳的英語單字了呢？

例如：

a. 有關手機的用語

cell phone （手機）	selfie stick （自拍棒）
wallpaper （桌布背景）	play on one's cell phone （玩手機／滑手機）
charging cable （充電線）	cell-phone number （手機號碼）
screen protector （保護貼）	roaming （漫遊）
earphones （耳機）	hotspot （熱點）

b. 有關辦公室的用語

bonus （紅利）	document （公文）
cabinet （檔案櫃）	company seal （公司印章）
calculator （計算機）	sick leave （病假）
computer （電腦）	writing desk （辦公桌）

d. 有關廚房的用語

bowl
（碗）

bread bin
（麵包箱）

dishcloth
（抹布）

dishwasher
（洗碟機）

draining board
（流理台）

oven
（烤箱）

scale
（秤）

tap
（水龍頭）

toaster
（烤麵包機）

washing machine
（洗衣機）

waste bin
（垃圾箱）

c. 有關蔬果菜餚的用語

apple
（蘋果）

banana
（香蕉）

bean
（豆莢）

cabbage
（包心菜）

carrot
（紅蘿蔔）

lemon
（檸檬）

mushroom
（蘑菇）

orange
（柳橙）

peach
（桃子）

pear
（梨）

3. 首尾聯想記憶法

所謂首尾聯想記憶法，就是掌握英語的造字規則，徹底掌握英文單字的來龍去脈，了解字首、字尾、字根代表的意義，英文單字倍數增加很容易喔！

如「un」是表「不」的字首，像這類的單字有 arm（武裝），unarm（解除武裝）；bend（彎曲）；unbend（使變直）；close（關閉）；unclose（打開）……。

例如：

a. 表形容詞的字尾

admirable
（可欽佩的）

lovable
（可愛的）

available
（可用的）

movable
（可動的）

eatable
（可吃的）

payable
（應付的）

b. 表數量變化的字首

biannual
（一年兩次的）

biweekly
（一週兩次的）

bicolor
（二色的）

bicycle
（自行車）

triangle
（三角形）

tricycle
（三輪車）

4. 慣用語記憶法

所謂慣用語記憶法，就是把約定俗成的常用慣用語，連在一起記，一次記牢它，不要分開來一個字一個字地記。

這種慣用語和中文的四字成語一樣，結合得很緊密，要注意的是，它們往往也都不是字面上的含義了。例如：can 是能夠的意思，help 是幫助的意思，但組成片語 can help 之後，就不是「能夠幫助」的意思，而是「能夠避免」的意思。

又如 in long run 和 in short run 這兩句慣用語，連在一起使用時，意思就不是長跑或短跑。前一個是終究、最後、從長遠看來；後一個是從短期看來、短期的意思。在英語裡，「長跑」實際上的單字是 long-distance race；短跑是 dash。

英語的慣用語還有很多，例如：

a. warrant quality
（品質保證）

b. market survey
（市場調查）

c. trial and error
（嘗試錯誤）

d. admission free
（免費入場）

e. travelers' check
（旅行支票）

f. savings deposit
（儲蓄存款）

g. time deposit
（定期存款）

h. current account
（活期存款）

如何把文法學好

在還沒有提到如何把文法學好之前，我們先來看看下面所列的兩個英文句子：

a. Mary put her money in her bag.

b. Mary put her money into her bag.

如果沒有對這兩個句子做文法上的分析，大概只能模糊地知道這兩句話的意思，沒辦法很清楚了解它們之間的區別，以及何時該用那一句。

這兩句英文主要的區別，是在介係詞 in 和 into 上。b 句表示「錢」轉移的全部過程，「瑪麗把錢放進口袋裡」；而 a 句指的則是過程的終結，「錢」存放在一個特定的地方，即「瑪麗把錢放在口袋裡」。

由此可知，大家應該可以明白文法的重要性了。

學文法，需要學好常見的詞類和句型。比如：五大基本句型、八大詞類、簡單句和複合句、動詞的語態和時態。等循序漸進學到一定階段，就可以找一本簡明的英文文法書，更有系統地學習文法知識。

不過要記得，學文法跟學發音、字彙不一樣，不需要去朗讀、背誦或默寫公式；而是要去理解，並對句子進行文法分析。所以，學文法要靠多想、多用，不要背誦，與其背文法，還不如背誦課文或句子。

當然也有些人認為要掌握英語，就只要學好文法，和盡可能多背單字就行了。這種文法加字彙的英語學習公式，使學生忽視了聽、說、讀、寫等四種能力的訓練。

學習文法和字彙，並不是我們學習英語的目的。即使學了英語，拿起英語資料看不懂，見到外國人說不出、聽不懂，文法學得再好，字彙記得再多也沒有用。更何況支離破碎的英語文法和字彙，是學不通，也記不住的。

所以，只有在聽、說、讀、寫的實際訓練過程中，彼此相互搭配學習，才能把文法真正學通，把單字真正記住。

聽的訓練

如何提高聽力？

提高聽力的方法見仁見智，不過，不管訓練方法是如何五花八門，大致都可以歸納為兩大類：精聽和泛聽。

精聽，注重聽懂每個句子，甚至每個單字。精聽的基本訓練方法是聽和寫，逐句逐句的聽，然後把每個單字都寫下來。

泛聽是把一篇材料，從頭到尾聽過去。開始訓練時可以多聽幾遍；隨著聽力的提高，逐漸減到三遍；最後減到一遍。聽完，一定要求能知道其內容大意。

精聽是聽力學習的基礎，泛聽是聽力訓練的目的。只重精聽，容易犯「只見樹木不見林」的毛病；泛聽強調聽懂大意，只重泛聽，容易忽略細節。在聽力訓練的初期，宜多注重精聽，減少泛聽。

隨著聽力的提高，逐漸減少精聽，增加泛聽，是一種很好而且合理的學習方式。

一般說來，聽力訓練最好從一分鐘 90 或 100 個字開始。以英語為母語的人，講話速度隨著當時環境和個人習慣，有很大的差異。正常情況下的速度約在每分鐘 150 ～ 170 字之間。

之前，我們較為熟知的四家英語廣播台的廣播速度如下：

ICRT：120w/min 左右

VOA 特別英語節目：90w / min 左右

VOA 正常節目：150 ～ 170w / min

BBC：150 ～ 180w / min

不過，也有人問：「有必要去聽 BBC、ICRT 和 VOA 嗎？」

如果不多練習聽力，怎麼和老外暢所欲言？我們發覺，有時甚至連那些常和老外直接接觸、共事，英語本就具有相當程度的人，也會覺得老外的英語並不容易聽懂。

究竟 BBC、ICRT 和 VOA 的新聞英語，是以多快的速度來播報的呢？一般而言，快一點的講話速度，大約一分鐘 175 字左右，十分清晰的演講，約是 125 ～ 160 字之間，而 ICRT 和 VOA 的新聞英語播報速度是 120 字（也就是五分鐘 600 字）。

VOA 最早關於速度比例的指示，是在 1928 年。當時以一分鐘 100 字為理想速度。時代改變，廣播設備大量更新，現在，獲世界高評價的廣播機構之一的 BBC，是以 120 字為基準。

美國傳播學者認為，一分鐘 120 字到 128 字之間的廣播速度過慢，應該介於 135 字到 140 字之間較為適當。更早以前，也有權威人士認為一分鐘在 165 字到 175 字之間較好。

所以，在日常生活中，英美人士以 BBC、ICRT 或 VOA 的新聞英語播報速度來談話，是十分平常的！

因此，透過電視和廣播，來訓練您的聽力，是提高聽力很好的訓練方式，不過，現在 YouTube 頻道，有很多英語教學節目，可以免費訓練英語的聽力，隨時隨地都可聽，儼然已經成為英語學習的主流。

只要懂得五大句型，就能說英語

學英語，要特別注意所謂的基本句型，這五種基本句型，可說是句子的骨架，以下，我們將再次複習這五種基本句型，將英語的規則性加以組合，讓大家了解其重要性，不管是說話或是寫文章，都要充分習慣它的用法。

第一種基本句型

S + V

這是由主詞（s）和動詞（v）所構成的最單純的句型。

s + v 常見的句型

- **I'll say !**

（當然！）

- **You bet ?**

（真的？）

- **Who cares !**

（誰稀罕！）

- **4That depends.**

（看情形！）

- **That will do.**

（沒有問題！）

- **You don't say ?**

（不是這樣嗎？）

- **Now you're talking.**

（這才正確！）

第二種基本句型

S + V + C

這是由主詞（s）、動詞（v）和補語（c）所形成的句子，因為必須加上補語，所以，這類動詞稱為不完全不及物動詞。

【例句】

✿ **My mother is a teacher.**

（我媽媽是老師。）

✿ **My brother became a writer.**

（我哥哥成了作家。）

s + v + c 常見的句型

✿ **That's great !**

（太棒了！）

✿ **That's life.**

（那才是人生。）

✿ **That's good news.**

（那是個好消息！）

✿ **That's too bad.**

（那真糟糕！）

第三種基本句型

S + V + O

這是由主詞（s）、動詞（v）和受詞（o）所構成的句型，動詞是完全及物動詞，後面不接補語，只接一個受詞。

【例句】

✿ **I love you.**

（我愛你。）

✿ **Mary speaks English very well.**

（瑪麗的英文說得很好。）

s + v + o 常見的句型

✿ **I'll miss you.**

（我會想念你。）

✿ **I don't mind it.**

（我不介意。）

✿ **Don't mention it.**

（不要客氣。）

✿ **Have a nice day !**

（祝你有愉快的一天。）

✿ **We had a very good time.**

（我們玩得很愉快。）

第四種基本句型

$S + V + O_1 + O_2$

這種句型在主詞和動詞的後面，接了兩個受詞，一個是直接受詞，一個是間接受詞，這種動詞稱為完全及物動詞。

【例句】

✿ **My daughter wrote a letter to me.**

（我的女兒寫了一封信給我。）

$S + V + O_1 + O_2$ 常見的句型

✿ **I wish you the same.**

（我也恭喜你。）

✿ **Would you do me a favor ?**

（能否幫我一個忙？）

✿ **I'll give you a ring soon.**

（我會儘快回你電話。）

第五種基本句型

$S + V + O + C$

這種句型是由主詞（s）、動詞（v）、受詞（o）和受詞補語（c）構成的，動詞是不完全及物動詞，後面加受詞補語。

這類動詞大致可以分為三類：

1. 使役動詞— make, set, keep, leave, choose..... 等。

2. 感官動詞— think, believe, find, feel, hear, see.... 等。

3. 意願、稱呼、判斷動詞— want, like, call, notice, declare... 等。

【例句】

✿ **We all wanted you to be happy.**

（我們都希望你快樂。）

s + v + o + c 常見的句型

✿ **Let your hair down.**

（放輕鬆一點。）

✿ **Don't get me wrong.**

（請不要誤會我。）

✿ **Please make yourself at home.**

（請不要拘束。）

說的訓練

如何提升說英語的能力？最重要的是膽子要大，敢於開口說話，而且心中要有一個假想的聽眾。如果心中只是想著文法，還沒有開口就擔心犯錯，嘴吧自然就打不開來了，最後的結果，就是永遠學不會說英語。

不過這裡要提醒您，如果光只是膽子大、敢開口，還是不夠的，應該要學些東西，做些練習。首先，要學習一些口語。英語在日常生活中有它特有的用語，例如：見面時如何打招呼，拿起電話怎麼說…等等。而且還要知道在不同的場合、不同的對象，所使用的各種英語。

例如，見面打招呼常用的習慣句有：

✿ **Hello.**

（哈囉。）

✿ **Hi.**

（嗨。）

✿ **Pleased to meet you.**

（很高興見到你。）

✿ **Glad to meet you.**

（很高興見到你。）

✿ **Nice to meet you.**

（見到你真好。）

✿ **How do you do ?**

（你好嗎？）

✿ **I'm very glad to meet you.**

（很高興見到你。）

✿ **It's a pleasure to meet you.**

（見到你是我的榮幸。）

✿ **How's the business ?**

（近來生意如何？）

✿ **It's been a long time.**

（好久不見了。）

✿ **How are you ?**

（你好嗎？）

✿ **How have you been ?**

（你好嗎？）

✿ **How are you doing ?**

（你好嗎？）

✿ **What's new ? / What's happening ?**

（有什麼新鮮事？）

✿ **Long time no see.**

（好久不見。）

✿ **I haven't seen you for ages. How are you ?**

（好久不見，你好嗎？）

同樣都是打招呼，但每句話有不同的親密程度。對長輩或新交的朋友，可以用 How do you do，但不可以用 Hi。

不過，僅僅記住一些習慣用語是不夠的。在一個場合，只講完幾句習慣用語，就沒有話說，是不行的。還是要有一定的表達方法，才能讓您的英語會話，說得流利，話題源源不絕。

讀的訓練

如何訓練閱讀能力呢？

a. 要掌握基本閱讀技巧

所謂的閱讀能力，並不是單純地指閱讀的速度，或一分鐘讀多少英語單字，而是除了速度，還要讀得懂。這是一體兩面的問題，要做到這些，就要有一定的閱讀技巧才行。

說到這裡，首先需要了解及確定自己閱讀的目的。是為了理論研究？為了取得特殊信息？還是為了消遣？沒有確定的閱讀目的，就不能充分發揮閱讀技巧。

當你在閱讀的時候，免不了會遇到生字，如何處理生字，就是一種閱讀技巧。不是所有的生字都必須查字典，而是視這個單字在句中或文章中的重要性而定，你可以做出下面四種不同的處理方式：（1）跳過去，（2）判斷詞義，（3）用構字法辨別生字，（4）查字典。

b. 提升閱讀速度

通常，對於一般題材、難度中等的文章，閱讀速度為每分鐘五十個單字；難度略低，生字不超總字數 2% 的材料，速度達到每分鐘九十個單字，理解準確率不低於 70%。

有關閱讀速度的問題，請先看下列的閱讀速度表：

每分鐘閱讀速度	評語
170 ～ 200 字	很慢
200 ～ 230 字	慢
230 ～ 250 字	一般
250 ～ 300 字	略高於一般
300 ～ 350 字	中等快速
350 ～ 450 字	快
450 ～ 550 字	很快
550 ～ 650 字	特別快

上面的閱讀速度表，是以英語為母語的人之閱讀速度標準。如果要對非英語系國家的人做這種要求，是不可能的，不過了解這張表，可以拿來做為努力的目標。

寫的訓練

如何提升寫作的能力？

英文寫作，一定要注意內容的連貫，有無重大的文法錯誤。

如果要做到內容連貫，首先要注意的是，寫文章時，心中一定要有讀者。

如果心中有讀者，寫文章時就會想到如何用讀者能理解的方法，把要說的事情說清楚，如果目的明確，內容就容易連貫。

當內容連貫之後，還要懂得段落發展的方法。通常，段落的發展有下面八種方法：因果法、推論法、舉例法、解釋法、比較法、描述法、對比法、分析法等等。

除了內容要連貫之外，還要注意文章的起、承、轉、合，也就是開頭、結尾和各段之間的相互關係。

當然，勤背英語諺語和成語，也可以讓您的寫作更流利，文字更優美、更洗鍊。這是提升寫作能力很好的一條捷徑。

下面八句，是您經常會看到的英語諺語：

✿ **Live and learn.**

（活到老學到老。）

✿ **Practice makes perfect.**

（熟能生巧。）

✿ **No pains, no gains.**

（一分耕耘，一分收穫。）

✿ **The early bird catches the worm.**

（早起的鳥兒有蟲吃。）

✿ **Easier said than done.**

（知易行難。）

✿ **Easy come, easy go.**

（來得快，去得也快。）

✿ **Where there is a will, there is a way.**

（有志者，事竟成。）

✿ **Knowledge is power.**

（知識就是力量。）

除此之外，當然您還可以多抄寫課文，用課文中的單字造句，甚至寫日記。把課文從英文譯成中文，再從中文譯成英文，單字經過反複使用，就會記得牢、用得活。另外，也可以做一些遊戲來複習單字，像接龍、填字遊戲等等。可以兩人做，也可以多人分組來做。

西洋諺語說「No pains, no gains.」，只要肯下功夫，你很快就會進入英語的殿堂了。

MEMO

Part 2
英語會話的第一步

Chapter 2 打開話匣子

How do you do？
（你好嗎？）

MP3-02

Dialog 1 客氣有禮的打招呼

A Mike, I'd like you to meet my brother, Tom.

（麥可，來見見我哥哥湯姆。）

B Pleased to meet you, Tom.

（湯姆，很高興見到你。）

C Nice to meet you, Mike.

（麥可，見到你真好。）

Dialog 2 客氣地打招呼、寒暄

A Hi, it's nice to meet you.

（嗨！很高興見到你。）

B I'm happy to meet you, too.

（我也很高興見到你。）

Jenny has told me a lot about you.

（珍妮常跟我提到你。）

A Only good things, I hope.

（希望都是好話。）

B Oh, yes.

（當然。）

She said you are pretty and smart.

（她說你既聰明又漂亮。）

Dialog 3 拘謹有禮的打招呼

A Mr. Lee, I'd like to introduce a friend of mine, Jane Lin.

（李先生，讓我介紹我的朋友，林珍妮。）

B I'm very glad to meet you, Miss Lin.

（很高興見到你，林小姐。）

C It's a pleasure to meet you.

（見到你是我的榮幸。）

Dialog 4 較輕鬆的打招呼

A Helen, this is my brother, Peter.

（海倫，這是我哥哥彼得。）

B How do you do, Peter ?

（你好，彼得。）

C Hello.

（哈囉！）

Dialog 5 更輕鬆的打招呼

A It's nice meeting you.

（很高興見到你。）

B Same here.

（我也是。）

Dialog 6 最隨便不拘禮的招呼

A Susan, this is Jack.

（蘇珊，這是傑克。）

B Hello.

（哈囉。）

C Hi.

（嗨。）

Dialog 7 老朋友好久不見

A I haven't seen you for ages.

（好久不見了。）

Where have you been ?

（你都到哪裡去了？）

B Yes. It's been quite a while.

（是有一段時間了。）

I've been abroad for the past months.

（我前幾個月一直在國外。）

Dialog 8 老友巧遇

A John！How are you？

（嗨！約翰，你好嗎？）

I haven't seen you for ages.

（好久不見。）

B Hi, Mary, how are you？

（嗨！瑪麗，你好嗎？）

Where are you going？

（你要去哪裡？）

A I'm on my way to work.

（我正要去上班。）

B Oh, I didn't know you were working.

（我不知道你在工作了。）

I thought you were studying at college.

（我以為你還在唸大學。）

A Oh, sure. This is only a part-time job.

（是啊，這個工作只是兼差的。）

Dialog 9 偶遇爸媽的朋友

A Oh, Mrs. Chang, it's been a long time.

（哦，張太太，好久了。）

How are you ?

（你好嗎？）

B Mary, it's been a long time.

（瑪麗，好久不見了。）

I'm fine, honey, and you ?

（我很好，甜心你呢？）

A Oh, pretty good.

（很好。）

Dialog 10 兩人見面打招呼

A Hi, haven't seen you in a while.

（嗨，好久不見。）

How have you been ?

（你好嗎？）

B Pretty good.

（很好。）

Look at you !

（看看你。）

Man, you've really gained weight, haven't you ?

（天啊！你胖了不少，是不是？）

A Yup.

（正是。）

Dialog 11 兩位鄰居打招呼閒聊

A Hi. What's new ?

（嗨，有什麼新鮮事？）

B Not much.

（沒什麼。）

A Wasn't that a great football game last night ?

（昨晚的足球賽是不是很棒？）

B Yup.

（是啊。）

Dialog 12 好朋友打招呼

A Hi, John. What's happening ?

（嗨，約翰。有什麼新鮮事？）

B Nothing. What's new with you ?

（沒什麼。你呢？）

Dialog 13 老朋友好久不見

A John ! How are you ?

（約翰，你好嗎？）

Long time no see.

（好久不見。）

B Yeah ! How have you been ?

（是啊！你好嗎？）

Dialog 14 平常打招呼

A Hi, John, how are you doing ?

（嗨！約翰，你好嗎？）

B Mary, how are you ?

（瑪麗，你好嗎？）

A O.K.

（還好。）

Where are you going ?

（你要去哪裡？）

B I'm going to the library.

（我要去圖書館。）

你一定要知道

通常，人與人見面，第一件事就是打招呼。不管是老朋友好久不見，上班同事見面，或是有人介紹你與別人見面，無時無刻你都在與人打招呼。不同的場合，親疏不同的人，都有不同的打招呼法，熟悉各種招呼法，你的人際關係會更無往不利。

精華短句濃縮篇

✎ 初見面時如何打招呼

✿ Hi.

（嗨。）

✿ Hello.

（哈囉。）

✿ How do you do ?

（你好嗎？）

✿ I'm very glad to meet you.

（很高興見到你。）

✿ It's a pleasure to meet you.

（見到你是我的榮幸。）

✿ Pleased to meet you.

（很高興見到你。）

✿ Glad to meet you.

（很高興見到你。）

✿ Nice to meet you.

（見到你真好。）

✎ 熟人之間的說法

✿ How are you ?

（你好嗎？）

✿ How's the business ?

（近來生意如何？）

✿ I haven't seen you for ages. How are you ?

（好久不見，你好嗎？）

✿ It's been a long time.

（好久不見了。）

✿ How have you been ?

（你好嗎？）

✿ How are you doing ?

（你好嗎？）

✿ What's new ? / What's happening ?

（有什麼新鮮事？）

✿ Long time no see.

（好久不見。）

✎ 正式拘禮的說法

A I'm very glad to meet you.

（很高興見到你。）

B It's a pleasure to meet you.

（見到你是我的榮幸。）

✎ 還算正式有禮的說法

A Pleased to meet you.

（很高興見到你。）

B Nice to meet you.

（見到你真好。）

✎ 較輕鬆的說法

A How do you do ?

（你好。）

B Hello.

（哈囉。）

✎ 最隨便不拘禮的用法

A Hello.

（哈囉。）

B Hi.

（嗨。）

✎ 較正式的說法

A I haven't seen you for ages.

（好久沒見到你了。）

B Yes, it's been quite a while.

（是啊，有一段時間了。）

✎ 舊識間很正式的打招呼

A Mike. It's been a long time.

（麥可，好久不見。）

How are you ?

（你好嗎？）

B Yes, it's been a long time.

（是啊！好久了。）

I'm fine, and you ?

（我很好，你呢？）

✎ 較不正式的說法

A Hi, haven't seen you in a while.

（好久不見。）

How have you been ?

（你好嗎？）

B Pretty good.

（很好。）

✎ 現在流行的打招呼法

A Hi, What's new ? / Hi, What's happening ?

（嗨，有什麼新鮮事？）

B Not much./ Nothing.

（沒什麼。）→（還是老樣子。）

✎ 很不正式的打招呼方式

A Hi, Mike, long time no see.

（嗨，麥可，好久不見。）

B Yeah.

（是啊！）

✎ 平常非正式的招呼語

A How are you doing ?

（你好嗎？）

B O.K.

（還好。）

Do you know where it is ?
（你知道它在那裡嗎？）

MP3-03

Dialog 1 在找洗衣店

A I was wondering if you know of a laundry shop in the neighborhood.

（你知道這附近有自助洗衣店嗎？）

B Gee, I'm sorry. I don't.

（很抱歉，我不知道。）

There is a laundry room in my apartment building, so I've never had to go outside for it.

（我們那棟公寓有洗衣房，所以我不必到外面的自助洗衣店。）

Dialog 2 找家便宜的餐廳

A I was wondering if you know of an inexpensive, but good restaurant.

（你知不知道有哪家餐廳物美價廉？）

B Oh, sure, there is one just around the corner.

（有，轉角就有一家。）

Dialog 3 在找健身房或俱樂部

A Could you tell me where I could find a gym or a health club ?

（你能不能告訴我，哪裡可以找到健身房或是健身俱樂部？）

B Yes, there is a gym in the recreation center.

（好啊，休閒中心裡就有健身房。）

Dialog 4 找銀行

A Would you know if there's a bank nearby ?

（你知道這附近有銀行嗎？）

I have to find one as soon as possible.

（我必須儘快去。）

B Actually, yeah, there's one right next to the "Kentucky Fried Chicken".

（有，「肯德基炸雞店」旁邊有一家。）

Dialog 5 要買舊傢俱

A Do you know where I can buy some used furniture ?

（你知道哪裡可以買到舊傢俱嗎？）

B I think you may try the garage sales.

（我想你可以到車庫拍賣會找找看。）

Dialog 6 找公用電話

A Do you know if there's a pay phone nearby ?

（你知道這附近有公共電話嗎？）

B I wish I could help you, but I really don't know.

（真希望我能幫上忙，但我真的不知道。）

Dialog 7 到店裡買東西

A Do you carry shower curtains ?

（你們店裡有賣浴簾嗎？）

B No, we don't.

（沒有。）

You may try the "Bath Mart."

（你可以到「浴室專賣店」問問看。）

A Do you know where it is ?

（你知道店在哪裡嗎？）

B No, I don't.

（不知道。）

But you can find the address in the yellow pages.

（但你可以在電話簿找到住址。）

你一定要知道

遇到不知道的事情，最好的方法就是開口問，如何問得好，別人才會樂意回答我們呢？就是你必需要掌握的竅門了。

✎ 最好的詢問方式

✿ I was wondering if you know~.

（我在想你是否知道～）

✿ Could you tell me~ ?

（你能不能告訴我～？）

✿ Would you know~ ?

（你是否知道～？）

✿ Do you know~ ?

（你是否知道～？）

✎ 客氣的詢問法

✿ I was wondering if you know~.

（你知不知道～）

✎ 很客氣的詢問法

✿ Could you tell me~ ?

（你能不能告訴我？）

✎ 比較不正式的詢問

✿ Would you know~ ?

（你知不知道～？）

✿ Do you know~ ?

（你知不知道～？）

3 Good-bye.
（再見）

實況會話

MP3-04

Dialog 1 結束一段對話

A Well, I'd better get going.

（啊，我得走了。）

I've got to get up early tomorrow.

（我明天一大早就要起床。）

B I'm so glad you could come.

（很高興你能來。）

I had a great time.

（今晚真愉快。）

A Me too. Thanks for inviting me.

（是啊！謝謝你的邀請。）

B My pleasure.

（那是我的榮幸。）

A See you later.

（再見。）

Dialog 2 到別人家做客

A Well, I'm afraid I have to be going.

（我該走了。）

B Thank you for coming.

（謝謝你的光臨。）

Dialog 3 在任何談話的場合

A It's been a pleasure.

（談得真愉快。）

B Yes, I've enjoyed it.

（是啊，我也很高興。）

Dialog 4 對方給你好的建議時用

A Thank you for the advice.

（謝謝你的建議。）

B My pleasure.

（那是我的榮幸。）

Dialog 5 表示談話愉快

A I really must go.

（我真的該走了。）

B Maybe we can talk again.

（那我們以後再聊。）

Dialog 6 表示談話愉快依依不捨

A Well, it's getting late.

（啊，這麼晚了。）

Maybe we could get together sometime.

（下次有機會再聊。）

B Sounds good.

（好啊！）

Dialog 7 用在平輩和朋友之間

A I've really got to go.

（我真的該走了。）

B OK, see you.

（好啊！再見。）

Dialog 8 用在平輩和朋友之間

A Got to go now.

（我得走了。）

B See you again.

（再見。）

你一定要知道

聊天時，要結束一段對話，也是談話當中很重要的一環，如何在一段愉快的談話之後，彼此留下美好印象；如何表達才能讓對方知道該結束了，是很重要的。因此說再見時，就不要一成不變的說 Good- bye.，此時，你的英文能力就見真章了。

Good night. 不僅僅是晚上睡覺前道晚安時用，凡是天天見面的同學、同事、朋友，大家在分手時，打算明天再見，當天不會再見面時，均可用 Good night.。

道別的俏皮話：「See you later, alligator」。alligator 是鱷魚，與 later 同押韻，美國的年輕人、小孩子喜歡這種俏皮的說法。

精華短句濃縮篇

✿ Good-bye.

（再見。）

✿ So long.

（再見。）→（離別時間較久）

✿ Farewell.

（再會。）

✿ Good-night.

（明天見。）→（睡前或下班）

✿ See you tomorrow.

（明天見。）

✿ See you later.

（待會見。）→（上班時）

✿ Take it easy.

（不要累到了。）

✿ Take care.

（再見。）

✎ 道別的說法

A Good night, Mary.

（明天見。）

B Good night, John.

（明天見。）

✎ 最一般性的說法

A Good-bye, John.

（再見。）

B Good-bye, Mary.

（再見。）

✎ 常用的說法

A Have a nice day. (evening / weekend......)

（祝你有個愉快的一天。）（晚上／週末……。）

B You, too.

（我也同樣祝福你。）

✎ 輕鬆的道別方式

A Talk to you later.

（以後再談。）

B Bye. Take it easy.

（再見，別太累囉。）

✎ 很輕鬆的道別方式

A See you later.

（再見。）

B So long. Take care.

（再見，保重。）

MEMO

Chapter 3 交際應酬

Could I ask a quick question ?

（我可以請教一下嗎？）

MP3-05

Dialog 1 問對方星期五是否有空

A Excuse me, Mr. Lee.

（對不起，李先生。）

B Yes, what can I do for you ?

（是，有什麼事嗎？）

A I was wondering if you'll be available Friday afternoon.

（請你星期五是否有空？）

Dialog 2 請對方開個門

A Excuse me, John.

（對不起，約翰。）

B Yes, what can I do for you ?

（是，有什麼事嗎？）

A Can you open the door for me ?

（你可否幫我開門？）

Dialog 3 在店裡，店員沒看到你

A Excuse me, Miss / Mr.

（對不起，小姐／先生。）

B Yes, may I help you ?

（是，有什麼吩咐？）

A Would you please show me the necklace in the window ?

（可否請你拿櫥窗裡的項鍊給我看看？）

Dialog 4 請對方幫忙

A Pardon me, Mr. Lin.

（對不起，林先生。）

B Yes ?

（有什麼事嗎？）

A Would you please help me with my project ?

（可否請你幫我做這個計劃？）

Dialog 5 在課堂上

A Professor Chang ?

（張教授？）

B Yes ?

（有什麼事嗎？）

A Could you tell us about the course requirements ?

（可否請您告訴我們這一科有什麼要求？）

Dialog 6 向服務生要賬單

A Waiter, check, please.

（服務生，我要結帳。）

B Sure. In a minute, ma'am.

（好，馬上來。）

Dialog 7 叫女服務生拿菜單

A Waitress ! We'd like a menu, please.

（服務生！我們要菜單。）

B Oh, I'm sorry. Here you are.

（噢，對不起，在這兒。）

Dialog 8 請問對方

A Excuse me, but could I ask a quick question ?

（對不起，我可以很快地問你一個問題嗎？）

B Sure. What can I do for you ?

（可以啊！什麼事？）

A Do you know if Jane sent the letter out yet ?

（你知道珍妮把那封信寄出去了嗎？）

Dialog 9 請問醫生

A Excuse me, but could I ask a quick question ?

（對不起，我可以請教一下嗎？）

B Sure.

（可以啊！）

A Will my mom be all right ?

（我媽媽會好嗎？）

Dialog 10 打斷大人的談話

A Mom, I'm sorry to interrupt you, but this is urgent.

（媽，很抱歉打斷你們的談話，但我有件很重要的事。）

B It's all right. What is it, dear ?

（沒關係，有什麼事？）

A Before I go to bed, I need you to sign the permission slip for the field trip tomorrow.

（在我睡覺前，必須先讓你簽這張家長同意書，我明天才可以去遠足。）

Dialog 11 想插嘴

A Am I interrupting ?

（我打斷你們的談話了嗎？）

B No, it's all right.

（沒有，沒關係。）

We're just talking.

（我們只是隨便閒聊而已。）

你一定要知道

如果，你想要跟別人講話時，有時對方正好沒看到你，你如何叫他，讓他知道你要跟他講話。或是對方在他的辦公室裡，你禮貌上先出個聲音，讓他知道你想跟他講話，英語常用的詞語，就是 Excuse me. 或 Pardon me.。

精華短句濃縮篇

✎ 叫對方，引起他的注意

✿ Sir ? / Ma'am ?

（這位先生？／這位女士？）

✿ Excuse me, Mr. Lin.

（對不起，林先生。）

✿ Pardon me, Miss Lee.

（對不起，李小姐。）

✿ Waiter ! / Waitress ! / Miss !

（服務生！）→（在餐廳叫服務生。）

✿ Hey, Mary.

（嗨！瑪麗。）→（用在熟朋友之間。）

✿ Excuse me.

（對不起。）→（你不知道對方的名字，但你要跟他說話。）

✿ Hey you ! / Hey !

（喂！）→（這是很沒禮貌的叫法，少用為妙。）

✎ 在課堂上發言前先叫老師

✿ Mr. Lin ?

（林先生？）

✿ Dr. Lin ?

（林博士？）

✿ Mrs. Lin ?

（林太太？）

✿ Miss Lin ?

（林小姐？）

✿ Professor Lin ?

（林教授？）

✿ Sir ? / Ma'am ?

（老師？）→（千萬別叫 Teacher。）

✎ 有人叫時，如何回答

✿ Yes ?

（有什麼事？）

✿ Yes, what can I do for you？

（有什麼事嗎？）

✿ Yes, may I help you？

（有什麼吩咐嗎？）

✿ Yeah？

（有什麼事？）→（用在熟朋友間。）

✿ What？

（幹嘛？）→（最不耐煩最粗魯的回答，不用為妙，請參照音檔裡的音調。）

✎ 在別人辦公室門口，講話前先說一聲打擾

✿ Excuse me, can I ask you a question？

（對不起，可以請教一下嗎？）

✿ Excuse me, have you got a minute？

（對不起，有時間嗎？）

✿ Excuse me, but could I ask you a quick question？

（對不起，我可不可以很快地問個問題？）

✎ 有人在你辦公室門口想跟你說話，你如何回答

✿ Sure, come on in.

（可以啊，進來吧！）

✿ Sure, what can I do for you ?

（可以啊，有什麼事嗎？）

✎ 打斷別人的說話，叫對方的說法

✿ I'm sorry to interrupt you, but I have to talk to you.

（很抱歉打斷你們的談話，但我有話必須跟你說。）

✿ I don't want to interrupt, but I have to talk to you.

（我不是有意打斷你們的談話，但我有話必須跟你說。）

✿ I hate to interrupt, but I have to talk to you.

（我不想打斷你們的談話，但我有話必須跟你說。）

✿ Am I interrupting ?

（我打斷你們的談話了嗎？）→（熟朋友間的用法。）

✎ 如何回答

✿ No, it's all right.

（沒關係。）

✿ It's all right. What can I do for you ?

（沒關係，有什麼事嗎？）

✿ It's OK. What is it ?

（沒關係，什麼事？）

✎ 很客氣的說法

A Excuse me, Mr. Lee.

（對不起，李先生。）

B Yes, what can I do for you ?

（是，有什麼吩咐嗎？）

✎ 很客氣的說法

A Pardon me, Miss Chen.

（對不起，陳小姐。）

B Yes ?

（有什麼事嗎？）

✎ 有問題問老師

A Professor Chang ? / Dr. Chang ?

（張教授／張博士？）

B Yes ?

（有什麼事嗎？）

✎ 引起對方注意

A Excuse me, but could I ask a quick question ?

（對不起，我可以很快地問你一個問題嗎？）

B Sure. What can I do for you ?

（可以啊！什麼事？）

✎ 打斷別人的說話

A I'm sorry to interrupt you, but this is urgent.

（很抱歉打斷你說話，但這件事很緊急。）

B It's all right. What can I do for you ?

（沒關係，有什麼事嗎？）

✎ 熟朋友間不拘禮的說法

A Am I interrupting ?

（我打斷了你們的談話嗎？）

B No, it's all right.

（沒關係。）

Can I borrow your car ?
（我可以借你的車嗎？）

MP3-06

Dialog 1 借一個 25 分的硬幣

A Have you got a quarter I could borrow ?

（你有沒有二十五分錢的硬幣？）

I need to make a phone call.

（我要打電話。）

B Let me see. Yes, I do. Here you are.

（我看看，有，拿去。）

A Do you know the number of directory assistance ?

（你知道查號台幾號嗎？）

B I'm sorry I don't know.

（很抱歉，我不知道。）

A Well, thanks for the quarter.

（好吧！謝謝你的二十五分錢。）

I'll pay you back as soon as I get some change.

（等我一有零錢就還你。）

Dialog 2 商借打火機

A You don't have a lighter, do you ?

（你有沒有打火機？）

B No, I don't.

（沒有。）

Dialog 3 商借打字機

A Could I borrow your typewriter ?

（打字機可以借我嗎？）

B I'm sorry, but I'm using it.

（對不起，我正在用。）

Dialog 4 商借摩托車

A Would you mind if I borrowed your motorcycle ?

（你介意我借你的摩托車嗎？）

B No, go ahead.

（不介意，拿去騎吧！）

Dialog 5 借錢

A I wonder if you could lend me twenty bucks.

（你可以借我二十元嗎？）

B I'm sorry, but I'm broke.

（很抱歉，我身上沒錢。）

Dialog 6 借二十五分硬幣

A Do you think you could lend me a quarter ?

（你可以借我一個二十五分錢硬幣嗎？）

B I'm sorry. but I'm out of it.

（很抱歉，我都用完了。）

Dialog 7 請朋友幫忙家庭作業

A Excuse me, John, I wonder if you could help me with my math homework.

（對不起，約翰。你能幫我做數學作業嗎？）

B Sure thing.

（當然可以。）

Dialog 8 請同事代打報告

A I was wondering if you'd type the paper for me.

（你是否可以幫我打這份報告？）

B I really wish I could, but I have to work.

（我真希望可以幫你的忙，但我有工作要做。）

Dialog 9 請同事幫忙看公文、備忘

A Could you check the memo that I wrote ?

（你能不能檢查一下我寫的備忘？）

I'm not sure I did it right.

（我不知道寫得可不可以。）

B Sure. Anything in particular you want me to check ?

（好啊，你要我特別注意什麼嗎？）

A Uh, see if my point is clear enough for everyone to understand.

（看看我的重點是不是大家都看得懂。）

B It looks fine to me.

（我看是沒問題。）

Dialog 10 請同事幫忙

A Oh, John, could you help me for a minute ?

（約翰，你可不可以幫我一下？）

I can't find the file on the inventory.

（我找不到存貨的檔案。）

B Sure. I'd be glad to.

（好啊，我很樂意。）

Dialog 11 請代送報告

A Would you send this report to Dr. Smith ?

（你可以送這份報告給史密斯博士嗎？）

B Sure.

（可以啊！）

Dialog 12 請把紙條給某人

A Would you give this note to Miss Chen when you see her ?

（你看到陳小姐時，請把紙條給她。）

B No problem.

（沒問題。）

Dialog 13 買份報紙回來

A Would you get a newspaper on your way home ?

（你回來時，可以順便買份報紙嗎？）

B Certainly.

（好。）

Dialog 14 媽媽對女兒

A Mary, I'd like you to help me with the laundry.

（瑪麗，我要你幫我一起洗這些衣服。）

B OK. mom.

（好。）

Dialog 15 經理對秘書

A I'd like you to put this letter on file.

（我要你把這封信歸檔。）

B Certainly.

（是。）

Dialog 16 去郵局

A Do you think you might stop by a post office ?

（你可以順道去一趟郵局嗎？）

B I could. What would you like ?

（可以，你要做什麼？）

A Could you mail this letter for me ?

（可不可以請你幫我寄這封信？）

B Sure, I'd be glad to.

（可以，我很樂意幫忙。）

Dialog 17 去修鞋店

A Do you think you might stop by a shoe-repair shop？

（你可以順道去趟鞋店嗎？）

B I'd like to, but I really don't think I'll have time.

（我很想去，但我不認為我有時間去。）

你一定要知道

在日常生活中，你可能會對別人提出要求、商借東西，或要求別人的幫忙。當你提出要求時，因對方跟你的交情，關係親疏不同，都有不同的講法。

在：「You don't have a lighter, do you？」或「Have you got a lighter？」這兩個問題中，你的回答有兩種，就是「有」跟「沒有」。

「Would you mind if I borrowed your car？」這是客氣的借東西說法，但要非常小心這種問句的回答。答No時，表示你不介意，也就是你答應借對方；答Yes時，表示你會介意，也就是你不答應。

要注意，美國人說「I'm broke.」，不一定是說他真的破產了，根據上下文，他可能是說他身上沒錢。

在「I was wondering if you'd do me a favor.」中，你可以把你想請對方幫忙的事，取代句中的「do me a favor」，明確表達你的要求。

「Sure thing.」是熟朋友間很輕鬆的回答方式，和「Sure.」意思一樣。

✎ 商借東西的說法

✿ Could I borrow your car ?

（我可以借你的車子嗎？）

✿ Have you got a lighter ?

（有打火機嗎？）

✿ You don't have a lighter, do you ?

（你有沒有打火機？）

✿ Would you mind if I borrowed your car ?

（你介意我借你的車子嗎？）

✿ I wonder if you could lend me ten bucks.

（你可以借我十塊錢嗎？）

✿ Do you think you could lend me ten bucks.

（你可以借我十塊錢嗎？）

✎ 答應對方的說法

✿ Sure.

（可以！）

✿ Yes, I do.

（我有。）

✿ Yes, of course.

（可以啊！）

✿ No, go ahead.

（沒關係，拿去用吧！）

✎ 不答應借對方的說法

✿ No, I don't.

（我沒有。）

✿ Yes, I do mind.

（我介意。）→（表示不借。）

✿ I'm sorry, but I'm using it.

（對不起，我正要用。）

✿ I'm sorry, but I'm out of it.

（很抱歉，我都用完了。）

✎ 請求幫忙的說法

✿ Excuse me. I wonder if you could do me a favor.

（對不起，可否幫我一個忙？）

✿ I was wondering if you'd do me a favor.

（可否幫我一個忙？）

✿ Could you do me a favor ? /Would you do me a favor ?

（可否幫我一個忙？）

✿ I'd like you to help me.

（希望你能幫我的忙。）

✿ Do you think you might go by a post office ?

（你可以順道去一趟郵局嗎？）

✎ 答應幫忙的說法

✿ O.K.

（好。）

✿ Certainly.

（當然可以。）

✿ Sure. / Sure thing.

（好啊！）

✿ No problem.

（沒問題。）

✿ I'd be glad to.

（我很樂意。）

✿ Yes, of course.

（當然可以。）

✎ 拒絕幫忙的說法

✿ I'm sorry, but I'm using it.

（很抱歉，我正在用。）

✿ I'm sorry, but I'm out of it.

（很抱歉，我用光了。）

✿ I'd like to, but I don't have time.

（我很願意，但我沒時間。）

✿ I'd really like to help you out, but I can't.

（我很樂意幫你忙，但我不行。）

✎ 用於很熟的人之間

A You don't have a lighter, do you ? / Have you got a lighter ?

（你有沒有打火機？）

B Yes. I do. / No, I don't.

（有。／沒有。）

✎ 很客氣的說法

A Could I borrow your car ?

（我可以借你的車子嗎？）

B Yes, of course. / I'm sorry, but I'm using it.

（好啊。／對不起，我正要用。）

✎ 客氣的說法

A Would you mind if I borrowed your car ?

（如果我要借用你的車子，你介意嗎？）

B No, go ahead. / Yes, I would.

（我不介意，你去開吧！／我會介意。〈表示不借〉）

✎ 用於上司對下屬，或是長輩對晚輩

A I'd like you to help me.

（希望你能幫我的忙。）

B O.K.

（好的。）

✎ 暗示對方你需要幫忙

A Do you think you might stop by a post office ?

（你可以順道去郵局一趟嗎？）

B I could. What would you like ? / I'd like to, but I don't have time.

（可以啊！你要做什麼？〈表示答應〉／我很想，但我沒有時間。〈表示拒絕〉）

I'd like to, but I can't.

（我很樂意，但我不行。）

MP3-07

Dialog 1 婉拒邀請

A Would you like to have dinner with me on Friday evening ?

（要不要星期五晚上跟我一起吃飯？）

B Thank you for your invitation but I've already got other plans.

（謝謝你的邀請，但我另外還有事。）

Dialog 2 婉拒去看電影的邀請

A How about going to a movie on Saturday ?

（星期六去看電影好嗎？）

B It's very nice of you to ask me.

（謝謝你的邀請。）

But I have to work.

（但那天我要工作。）

A Perhaps another time.

（那下次吧！）

Dialog 3 婉拒邀請

A Do you want to come over to dinner tonight ?

（你今晚要過來吃晚飯嗎？）

B I'm sorry. But I have another invitation.

（對不起，我另外有約了。）

Dialog 4 拒絕借東西給別人

A I was wondering if I could borrow the atlas.

（你可不可以把地圖借我？）

B I'd like to, but I'm using it now.

（我很願意，但我現在正在用。）

Maybe later.

（待會兒好了。）

A Oh, that's O.K. Thanks anyway.

（沒關係，謝謝。）

Dialog 5 拒絕送對方回去

A Would you please give me a ride home ?

（你可以開車送我回家嗎？）

B I'd like to, but I have to pick up my wife at the airport.

（我很願意，但我必須去機場接我太太。）

Dialog 6 拒絕借車給對方

A Would you mind if I borrowed your car ?

（我可以借你的車嗎？）

B Well, it really depends on when.

（那要看你何時要借。）

A Oh, just this weekend.

（這個週末。）

B I'm sorry, but it's just not possible.

（對不起，恐怕不行。）

Dialog 7 拒絕對方開出的價錢

A I'm sorry. I'm afraid I can't accept the deal with the price.

（對不起，那樣的價錢我無法接受。）

B Are you sure you won't change your mind ?

（你確定你不會改變心意嗎？）

Dialog 8 拒絕借住

A I was wondering if you'd let me stay with you for a few days.

（我可否在你這兒住幾天？）

B I'm sorry. I'm afraid it's not suitable.

（對不起，恐怕不方便。）

A Why not ? I'll leave as soon as I find an apartment.

（為何不行？我一找到公寓就離開。）

B I'd really like to help you out, but I don't think it's very proper.

（我很樂意幫你的忙，但我認為那不妥。）

你一定要知道

拒絕有兩種情形，一種是別人對你提出邀請，你拒絕他；另一種是別人要求你幫忙，你拒絕他，要怎麼委婉拒絕，才不會傷到人心，這可要高明的技巧喔！

✎ 拒絕邀約的說法

✿ I appreciate your asking me, but I'm busy.

（謝謝你的邀請，但我很忙。）

✿ It's very nice of you to invite me, but I have another invitation.

（謝謝你的邀請，但我已接受別人的邀請。）

✿ Thank you for inviting me, but I've already got other plans.

（謝謝你的邀請，但我另外有事。）

✎ 拒絕別人提出的要求

✿ I'm sorry, but I'm using it.

（很抱歉，但我正在用。）

✿ I'm sorry. I'm afraid I can't accept it.

（很抱歉，我恐怕不能接受。）

✿ I'd like to, but I can't.

（我很樂意，但我不行。）

✎ 拒絕別人的好意

✿ Thank you for your offer, but I don't need it.

（謝謝你的好意，但我不需要。）

✎ 對於別人的拒絕如何回答

✿ Perhaps another time.

（那就下回吧！）

✿ Are you sure you won't change your mind ?

（你確定不會改變心意？）

✿ Oh, come on. Don't let me down.

（別這樣，別令我失望。）→（用於熟朋友之間。）

✎ 婉拒別人的邀請

A Thank you for your invitation, but I've already got other plans.

（謝謝你的邀請，但我已有其他的計劃。）

B Perhaps another time, then.

（那就下次吧！）

MEMO

I like your shirts.
（我喜歡你的襯衫。）

MP3-08

Dialog 1 稱讚對方的襯衫

A That's a nice shirt !

（你的襯衫很不錯！）

B Is it really OK ?

（真的嗎？）

A Yes, and I like the color, too.

（顏色也很好。）

It matches your tie.

（很配你的領帶。）

B I'm glad you have the same taste as mine.

（很高興你和我的品味一樣。）

Dialog 2 稱讚對方的報告

A That was a great report !

（那篇報告很棒！）

B You like it ?

（你喜歡嗎？）

A Yes, I was really impressed by your research.

（是，我對你的研究印象很深刻。）

B Thanks, I'm happy to hear it .

（謝謝，很高興聽你這麼說。）

Dialog 3 稱讚對方的車子

A Gee, what a pretty car !

（哇！好漂亮的車子！）

B I am glad you like it.

（很高興你喜歡。）

A How does she drive ?

（開起來怎麼樣？）

B Like a dream.

（就像我夢想的。）

Dialog 4 稱讚對方寫的書

A I read the book you wrote.

（我讀了你寫的書。）

It was wonderful.

（很棒！）

B Thank you. I'm glad you liked it.

（謝謝，很高興你喜歡。）

Dialog 5 稱讚對方的髮型

A I like your new hair style.

（我喜歡你的新髮型。）

B Thanks, do you really like it ?

（謝謝，你真的喜歡嗎？）

A Yes, sure. Where did you have it cut ?

（是啊，你在哪裡做的頭髮？）

B Do you know the famous hairstyler Tom at "Make You Pretty" beauty salon.

（你知不知道那家叫「使你漂亮」的美容院，有一位很有名的髮型師叫湯姆？）

A Yes, I heard about him.

（我聽說過他。）

Dialog 6 稱讚對方的皮包

A I love your purse.

（我好喜歡你的皮包。）

It's so pretty.

（真漂亮。）

B Oh, thank you.

（噢！謝謝你。）

My husband bought it in Tokyo last week.

（我先生上星期在東京買的。）

Dialog 7 稱讚對方的表演

A Your performance was just wonderful !

（你的表演真棒。）

B That's very kind of you.

（你真客氣。）

A I mean it quite sincerely.

（我是肺腑之言。）

B I'm glad to hear that.

（很高興聽你這麼說。）

Dialog 8 稱讚對方的洋裝

A What a beautiful dress !

（好漂亮的洋裝。）

B Oh, thanks, I like it, too.

（謝謝，我自己也很喜歡。）

Dialog 9 稱讚對方的套裝

A What a beautiful suit !

（好漂亮的套裝。）

The style is flattering on you.

（這個樣式你穿起來真好看。）

B You like it ?

（你真的喜歡嗎？）

你一定要知道

人與人之間的交往，多稱讚對方幾句是絕不吃虧的。但被稱讚時，可別傻傻地只會說 Thank you.，多加一句，就有畫龍點睛的效果，，談話才會生動。

在「That's a nice shirt !」這句英語中，shirt 可用任何一樣你要稱讚的字代替。

同樣的，在「Your performance was just wonderful.」中，performance 可用任何你要稱讚的東西代替。

精華短句濃縮篇

✎ 稱讚別人的說法

✿ What a beautiful blouse !

（好漂亮的上衣！）

✿ That's a very nice shirt !

（那件襯衫很好看！）

✿ I like your shirt.

（我喜歡你的襯衫。）

✿ Your performance was just wonderful.

（你的表演真棒。）

✿ I'm really impressed.

（令我印象深刻。）

✎ 如何回答他人的稱讚

✿ Do you really like it ?

（你真的喜歡嗎？）

✿ You liked it ?

（你真的喜歡？）

✿ Is it really O.K. ?

（真的可以嗎？）

✿ Oh, thanks, I like it, too.

（謝謝，我自己也很喜歡。）

✿ Glad you like it.

（很高興你會喜歡。）

✿ I'm glad to hear it.

（很高興聽你這麼說。）

✿ That's very kind of you.

（你真客氣。）

✎ 熟朋友之間

A I like your suit.

（我喜歡你的西裝。）

B Thanks, do you really like it ?

（謝謝，你真的喜歡嗎？）

✎ 稱讚對方

A That's a nice shirt !

（你的襯衫很不錯！）

B Is it really O.K. ?

（真的不錯嗎？）

✎ 一般用法

A What a beautiful blouse !

（好漂亮的上衣！）

B Oh, thanks, I like it, too.

（謝謝，我自己也很喜歡。）

✎ 一般用法

A Your performance was just wonderful !

（你的表演真的好棒！）

B That's very kind of you.

（你真客氣。）

Thank you.

（謝謝。）

MP3-09

Dialog 1 謝謝朋友送禮物

A Here, it's for you.

（這個，送你的。）

B Oh, thank you. It's wonderful, but you shouldn't have.

（噢，謝謝。好棒，但你不必這麼做的。）

A Well, I just wanted to show you how much I appreciated your kindness.

（嗯，我只是想讓你知道，我很謝謝你對我那麼好。）

Dialog 2 謝謝朋友的幫忙

A Thank you for your help.

（謝謝你的幫忙。）

B Well, what are friends for ?

（朋友是做什麼用的？）

Dialog 3 謝謝朋友

A Oh, thank you. But you really didn't have to.

（謝謝，但你實在不必這麼做。）

B But I wanted to.

（但我想這麼做。）

Dialog 4 謝謝朋友送玫瑰花

A Oh, thank you !

（噢，謝謝你。）

I just love roses.

（我最愛玫瑰花了。）

B I'm glad you like them.

（我很高興你喜歡。）

Dialog 5 謝謝朋友送風景照片

A It's beautiful ! Thank you very much.

（好漂亮，謝謝你。）

I've always wanted a picture of Yellow Stone National Park.

（我一直想要有一張黃石公園的照片。）

Did you get it in America ?

（你在美國買的嗎？）

B Yes, I bought it when I was in the United States.

（是啊，我去美國的時候買的。）

Dialog 6 謝謝朋友載你回家

A Thank you for driving me home.

（謝謝你載我回家。）

B My pleasure.

（那是我的榮幸。）

Let me know if you need a ride any time.

（你若需要有人載你，隨時告訴我。）

Dialog 7 謝謝別人的稱讚

A That's a nice tie.

（很不錯的領帶。）

B Oh, thanks. Is it really nice ?

（謝謝，真的不錯嗎？）

A You're a good driver.

（你的開車技術很好。）

B Thank you. And it's my pleasure to serve you.

（謝謝你，很榮幸為你服務。）

Dialog 8 謝謝別人的祝福

A Good luck on your exam tomorrow.

（祝你明天考得好。）

B Thank you. I'll need it.

（謝謝，我需要你的祝福。）

Dialog 9 離開宴會時，謝謝主人

A Thank you so much for the lovely evening.

（今晚真棒，謝謝你。）

I had a good time.

（我玩得很愉快。）

B Thank you for coming, I've been looking forward to seeing you for a long time.

（謝謝你能來，我一直期待能看到你。）

Dialog 10 謝謝別人提議幫忙

A Do you need help moving this weekend ?

（這個週末，要我幫你搬家嗎？）

B Thanks, but I've got four other guys.

（謝謝，但我已找到四個人了。）

Thanks for offering.

（謝謝你提議要幫忙。）

A Do you need help with your homework ?

（需要我幫忙你做功課嗎？）

B No, thank you. I'll manage it myself.

（不，謝謝你，我自己應付得來。）

Dialog 11 你要的桌燈朋友買不到

A I tried to buy those lamps you wanted so much, but they only had these really ugly ones left. Sorry.

（我想買你喜歡的那種桌燈，但店裡只剩下幾個這麼醜的，很抱歉。）

B Oh, that's O.K. Thanks for trying.

（沒關係，還是謝謝你。）

A Sorry, it's not what you expected.

（很抱歉，不是你想要的。）

Dialog 12 謝謝邀請，但沒法去

A Can you come over for dinner on Friday evening ?

（星期五晚上要不要過來吃晚飯？）

B I'd love to, but I've got other plans.

（我很想去，但我另外有事。）

Thanks anyway for the invitation.

（謝謝你的邀請。）

你一定要知道

說謝謝的場合很多，如何用英文得體地表達，是很重要的。別人對你說謝謝時，也該根據情況去應對才不會失禮。

中文的謝謝，英文是 Thank you.，這是最通俗的說法，但在 Thank you. 之後，再加上一、兩句，會讓整個對話生動起來。

精華短句濃縮篇

✎ 說謝謝

✿ Thank you. / Thank you. I appreciate it.

（謝謝。）

✿ I'm very grateful.

（我很感激。）

✿ I can't thank you enough.

（實在感激不盡。）

✿ Thank you, but you shouldn't have.
Thank you, but you really didn't have to.

（謝謝，但你實在不需要這麼做。）

✎ 回答別人的道謝

✿ You're welcome.
Not at all.
Don't mention it.

（別客氣。）

✿ My pleasure.

（我的榮幸。）

✿ No problem.

（沒問題。）

✿ Don't worry about it.

（沒什麼啦。）

✎ 雖然對方沒幫上忙，還是謝謝對方

✿ Thank you for trying.

（謝謝你的幫忙。）

✿ Thanks, anyway.

（無論如何，謝謝。）

✎ 回答雖然你幫不上忙，對方還是謝謝你

✿ Sorry, it didn't work out.

（對不起，事情沒做成。）

✿ Sorry, it's not what you expected.

（對不起，不是你所期待的。）

✎ 沒能真正幫上忙

A Thank you for trying.

（謝謝你盡你所能了。）

B Sorry, it didn't work out.

（很抱歉沒做成。）

A Thanks, anyway.

（無論如何，很感謝你。）

B Sorry, it didn't work out.

（很抱歉沒做成。）

✎ 很感動的說法

A Thank you, but you shouldn't have.

（謝謝，但你實在不需要這麼做。）

B Don't worry about it.

（沒什麼啦。）

A Thank you, but you really didn't have to.

（謝謝，但你實在不需要這麼做。）

B What are friends for ?

（朋友做什麼用的？）

✎ 通俗的說法

A Thank you.

（謝謝你。）

B You're welcome.

（不客氣。）

A Thank you.

（謝謝你。）

My pleasure.

（是我的榮幸。）

I am very sorry.

（我很抱歉。）

實況會話

MP3-10

Dialog 1 向朋友借的書丟了

A I'm sorry, but I can't find the book you lent me.

（很抱歉，但我找不到你借我的書。）

B It's all right.

（沒關係。）

A I can buy a new one for you.

（我可以買一本新的還你。）

B It's really O.K.

（真的沒關係。）

A Thanks for being so understanding.

（謝謝你這麼善體人意。）

Dialog 2 上課遲到

A I'm sorry I was late for class, Dr. Lee, but I overslept.

（很抱歉我上課遲到了，李教授，我睡過頭了。）

B Well, it's O.K. this time.

（這次沒關係。）

A Thanks, I won't let it happen again.

（謝謝，不會有下次了。）

Dialog 3 打電話取消約會

A Hello, John. Listen, I'm having a bit of trouble with the car, so I don't think I can make it tonight.

（嗨，約翰。我的車子有點毛病，我今晚不能來了。）

I'm really sorry.

(很抱歉。)

B Oh, really, what's wrong with it ?

(真的？是什麼毛病？)

A I don't know. I just can't start it.

(我也不知道，反正就是沒辦法發動。)

B I'll come over to your apartment.

(我過去你的公寓看看。)

A Thanks.

(謝謝。)

Dialog 4 撞到別人

A Oh, I'm sorry.

(噢，對不起。)

B Yeah. It's O.K.

(沒關係。)

I understand completely.

（我可以諒解。）

It's so crowded here.

（這裡好擠。）

Dialog 5 踩到別人的腳

A Oops, sorry. I didn't mean to.

（唉呀，對不起。我不是故意的。）

B It's all right.

（沒關係。）

Dialog 6 坐了別人的位子

A Oh, sorry. I didn't know you were sitting here.

（噢，對不起。我不知道你剛剛坐在這兒。）

Let me move my stuff to another table.

（我移一下我的東西到別張桌子。）

B No, it's O.K. There are still a lot of seats I'll move.

（不必了，沒關係，還有很多位子，我換位。）

Dialog 7 打翻咖啡

A I'm sorry about spilling coffee on the carpet.

（很抱歉，我打翻了咖啡，灑在地毯上了。）

B Oh, don't worry about it.

（沒關係。）

A I feel terrible.

（我很難過。）

Is there anything I can do ?

（有沒有什麼可以補救的辦法？）

B Just forget about it.

（別管它了。）

Dialog 8 說話傷到別人

A I'm sorry. I didn't mean to hurt your feelings.

（對不起，我不是故意傷你的心。）

B I understand it completely.

（我完全了解。）

Dialog 9 對鄰居的抱怨說對不起

A Hi, John. I hate to bring this up, but that new stereo system you got......

（嗨，約翰，我很不想說，但你新買的音響……）

B Yes ?

（怎麼啦？）

A You were playing it very late last night.

（你昨晚開到很晚。）

B Oh, I'm sorry.

（哦，對不起。）

I didn't realize that it bothered you.

（我不知道會吵到你。）

你一定要知道

平常人與人之間的交往，總會有不小心得罪人的時候。不小心做了什麼事，必須道歉的情況是常常會發生的，表達得體一切又會和好如初，可見得體的說話，是多麼重要。

精華短句濃縮篇

✎ 道歉的話

✿ Sorry about that.

（很抱歉。）

✿ I'm sorry, I didn't mean to.

（很抱歉，我不是故意的。）

✿ I can't tell you how sorry I am.

（對你的歉意筆墨難以形容。）

✿ I'm sorry. I didn't realize that it bothered you.

（很抱歉，沒想到會吵到你。）

✿ I hope you'll forgive me.

（希望你能原諒我。）

✎ 別人向你道歉時如何回答

✿ It's O.K.

（沒關係。）

✿ Oh, don't worry about it.

（別擔那個心。）

✿ Forget it.

（算了吧！）

✿ It's all right.

（沒關係。）

✿ No problem.

（沒問題的。）

✿ I understand it completely.

（我很了解。）

簡單會話

✎ 最基本的說法

A I'm very sorry.

（我很抱歉。）

B It's all right.

（沒關係。）

MEMO

Part 3
英語會話的第二步

Chapter 4 社交英語

How are you today？
（你今天好嗎？）

MP3-11

Dialog 1

A Good afternoon！

（午安！）

How are you today？

（你今天好嗎？）

B Fine，thank you. And you？

（很好，謝謝。你呢？）

A Busy, but good.

（很忙，但是很好。）

B How is work going ?

（工作怎麼樣？）

A You know same old thing, just more of it these days.

（你知道的，還不是就那樣，只是這幾天又忙了點。）

B Well, good to see you.

（嗯，很高興見到你。）

Take care.

（保重。）

Dialog 2

A Oh my goodness, I haven't seen you in years.

（哦，天啊！我好多年沒看到你了。）

B I know.

（我知道。）

The last time I saw you, your son was in high school.

（上次我見到你，你公子還在唸高中。）

A How are you doing ?

（你好嗎？）

B I am great, thanks.

（我很好，謝謝你。）

A It was nice seeing you again.

（很高興再看到你。）

Take care.

（保重。）

Dialog 3

A How nice to see you !

（很高興見到你！）

What a pleasant surprise.

（真讓我驚喜！）

B How long has it been ?

（多久沒見面了？）

You look great.

（你看起來很好。）

A It has been years.

（好多年了。）

Thanks, you look great, too.

（謝謝你，你看起來也很好。）

B How's your family ?

（你的家人好嗎？）

A They are fine, thanks.

（他們很好，謝謝你。）

B I've really got to go.

（我真的該走了。）

Talk to you later.

（以後再聊。）

你一定要知道

與人打招呼問好時，有時會遇到對方既問你問題，同時又稱讚你氣色很好，讓你不知道該從何答起。這時候別緊張，你可以慢條斯理的先回答對方的問題，然後再謝謝對方的稱讚。例如：對方說「How long has it been ?」（我們多久沒見面了？）又說「You look great.」（你氣色很好。），你的回答就是：「It has been years. Thanks, you look great, too.」（有好多年了。謝謝，你看起來也很好。）

✎ 和人打招呼

A How are you doing ?

（您好嗎？）

B Great and yourself ?

（很好，您呢？）

✎ 問候對方的家人

A How is the family ?

（你的家人好嗎？）

B They are doing great, thanks.

（他們都很好，謝謝您。）

✎ 好久不見的招呼語

A How long has it been since I last saw you ?

（自從我上一次見到你，有多久了？）

B It has been at least a year.

（至少一年了。）

✎ 代為問候對方家人

A It was great seeing you again.

（很高興再見到氣。）

B Same here, tell the family hello.

（我也是，向你的家人問好。）

✎ 詢問對方工作情形

A Are you still working downtown ?

（你還在市中心上班嗎？）

B Yes and busy as ever.

（是的，而且一樣的忙。）

重點單字片語

- ☐ goodness [ˈgʊdnɪs] 天哪，啊呀（驚嘆語）
- ☐ pleasant [ˈplɛznṭ] 愉快的
- ☐ surprise [sɚˈpraɪz] 驚喜
- ☐ pleasure [ˈplɛʒɚ] 令人高興的事
- ☐ downtown [ˈdaʊnˈtaʊn] 商業區
- ☐ take care 保重

Excuse me.
（對不起。）

MP3-12

Dialog 1

A Excuse me, are you finished ?

（對不起，您看完了嗎？）

B Yes, you can take it.

（是的，你可以拿去。）

A Anything interesting in the news today ?

（今天有沒有什麼好看的新聞？）

B Yes, you should read the article on the front page about the plane crash.

（有啊，你應該看看頭版有關墜機事件的文章。）

A How terrible !

（真可怕！）

B I know.

（對啊！）

I prefer the bus myself.

（還好我只喜歡搭公車。）

Dialog 2

A Excuse me, where is the restroom ?

（對不起，請問洗手間在哪裡？）

B The closest one is near the shoe department.

（最近的一間靠近賣鞋子的部門。）

A Where is the shoe department ?

（賣鞋子的部門在哪裡？）

B Take the escalator to the fifth floor.

（搭電梯到五樓。）

Then take a left .

（然後向左轉。）

It is on the right hand side.

（洗手間就在右手邊。）

A Thanks for your help.

（謝謝您的幫忙。）

B No problem.

（沒問題。）

Have a nice day.

（祝您有美好的一天。）

Dialog 3

A Excuse me, is anyone sitting here ?

（對不起，這裡有人坐嗎？）

B No, have a seat.

（沒有，請坐。）

A Do you recommend anything on the menu ?

（你會推薦菜單上的什麼菜？）

B Yes, try the fried shrimp.

（你可以試試炸蝦。）

It is great.

（那很棒。）

A Thanks for the suggestion.

（謝謝你的建議。）

I will try it.

（我會試試看。）

你一定要知道

如果你有事要問別人或是會打擾到別人，都要先說一句 Excuse me.。例如：你想要問「洗手間在哪裡？」、「這個座位有沒有人坐？」、「你報紙看完了沒有？」、「表演開始了沒？」等等，都要用 Excuse me. 開頭。Excuse me. 表面上的意思是「對不起」，其實是起頭語，先說 Excuse me.，對方就知道你要跟他說話了。

若你在走路時，剛好有人擋住你的去路，你要請對方讓路、借過，說 Excuse me.，對方就會知道你要請他讓路。

Excuse me. 跟 I'm sorry. 的意思不一樣，I'm sorry. 是真的在向對方表示歉意。例如：有人跟你問路，而你也不知道，你覺得很抱歉，就要說 I am sorry.。

再見的英語說法很多，Have a nice day. 或 Have a nice evening. 也是其中的說法之一，翻譯成中文就是：「祝你有愉快的一天。」或「祝你有一個愉快的晚上。」雖然中國人很少這麼說，但美國人常在道別時使用。

✎ 詢問表演時間

A Excuse me, how long ago did the show start ?

（對不起，這個表演開始多久了？）

B Only a few minutes ago, you haven't missed anything.

（剛開始幾分鐘，你沒有錯過什麼。）

✎ 問飯店在哪裡

A Excuse me, I am looking for the Holiday Inn.

（對不起，我在找假日旅館。）

B I'm sorry, I am not familiar with the area.

（對不起，我對這一區並不熟。）

✎ 找座位

A Excuse me, is this seat taken ?

（對不起，這個座位有人坐嗎？）

B Yes, my husband went to the concession stand.

（有，我先生到零食販賣處去了。）

✎ 要報紙

A Excuse me, are you finished with the paper ?

（對不起，你報紙看完了嗎？）

B Yes, you can take it.

（是的，你可以拿去。）

✎ 找洗手間

A Excuse me, where is the closest ladies' room ?

（對不起，最近的女用洗手間在哪裡？）

B Third floor on the right.

（在三樓右邊。）

重點單字片語

- ☐ familiar [fəˈmɪljɚ] 熟悉
- ☐ area [ˈɛrɪə] 地區
- ☐ concession stand [kənˈsɛʃən ˌstænd] 零食販賣處
- ☐ closest [ˈklosɪst] 最接近的
- ☐ ladies' room 女用洗手間
- ☐ seat [sit] 座位
- ☐ article [ˈɑrtɪkl̩] 文章
- ☐ front [frʌnt] 前面

- ☐ plane [plen] 飛機
- ☐ crash [kræʃ] 撞毀
- ☐ terrible [ˈtɛrəbl̩] 可怕的
- ☐ prefer [prɪˈfɝ] 較喜歡
- ☐ department [dɪˈpɑrtmənt] 部門
- ☐ escalator [ˈɛskəˌletɚ] 電梯
- ☐ recommend [ˌrɛkəˈmɛnd] 推薦
- ☐ suggestion [səˈdʒɛstʃən] 建議
- ☐ have a seat 坐下
- ☐ be familiar with 對～熟悉
- ☐ restroom 洗手間

MEMO

Nice to meet you.
（很高興認識你！）

MP3-13

Dialog 1

A Hello, nice to meet you. I am Jane.

（哈囉，很高興認識你，我叫珍妮。）

B Nice to meet you as well. I am Robert.

（我也很高興認識你，我叫羅勃。）

A Have you been a member of the club long ?

（你成為這個俱樂部的會員很久了嗎？）

B Yes, for the past five years.

（是的，過去五年都是。）

A It is such a beautiful place.

（這個地方很好。）

B I know.

（沒錯。）

They keep the grounds in great condition here.

（他們把這裡草地的狀況保持得很好。）

Dialog 2

（A：Bob　B：Helen　C：Tom）

A Hi, Tom, I would like you to meet my wife, Helen.

（嗨，湯姆，來見見我太太海倫。）

B Hi, nice to meet you.

（嗨，很高興認識你。）

I've heard so much about you.

（我早就聽過很多關於你的事。）

C All good I hope.

（我希望全是好的。）

B Yes, Bob says you like to play golf.

（對啊，鮑伯說你很喜歡打高爾夫球。）

C Yes, I love it.

（是的，我很喜歡。）

I play as often as possible.

（只要一有時間，我就會去打。）

A We will have to play golf sometime.

（有空我們應該一起去。）

Dialog 3

（A ：Gary　B ：Jessica　C：Robert）

A Jessica, I'd like you to meet my friend, Robert Chen.

（潔西卡，來見見我的朋友陳羅勃。）

B Nice to meet you, Mr. Chen.

（陳先生，很高興認識你。）

C The pleasure's mine.

（那是我的榮幸。）

But call me Robert. Everyone does.

（叫我羅勃就好，大家都這麼叫。）

Mind if I call you Jessica ?

（你介意我叫你潔西卡嗎？）

B Of course not.

（當然不。）

But just plain "Jessie " will do.

（你可以只叫我潔西。）

Dialog 4

（A ：Tomas　B ：Jane　C：Henry）

A I would like you to meet my son, Henry.

（見見我的兒子亨利。）

B Hello, Henry, I am Jane.

（哈囉，亨利，我是珍妮。）

C My father says you are a baseball fan.

（我父親說你是一個棒球迷。）

B Yes, the Red Sox are my favorite team.

（是的，紅襪隊是我最喜歡的隊伍。）

C Really, I am a Yankee fan myself.

（真的，我自己是洋基隊迷。）

B We will have to go to a game sometime.

（有時間我們可以一起去看比賽。）

你一定要知道

一般英語會話書，都把「How are you ?」和「How do you do ?」翻譯成「你好嗎？」因此，初學英語者都以為這兩句話的用法一樣。其實這兩句話使用的場合完全不同，一定要分清楚，以免鬧笑話。

朋友把你介紹給其他人認識時，兩個被介紹的人彼此問候對方，要說「How do you do ?」（久仰久仰。），而不是說「How are you ?」

當有人介紹你跟另外一個人認識時，你們兩個被介紹的人，除了說「How do you do ?」以外，也可以說「Nice to meet you.」（很高興認識你）或「I've heard so much about you.」（別人常跟我提起你）這一類的話。

「How are you ?」是一句單純問好的話，不管是彼此認識不認識，平常都可以用「How are you ?」來打招呼，卻不可當作有人介紹你跟別人認識時的問候語。

一般來說，老外在彼此關係仍屬生疏時，會稱呼對方Mr.（先生）、Mrs.（太太）及Miss（小姐）。等到彼此較為熟識，才會直接稱呼對方的名字。但是當有人介紹你跟另外一個人認識時，為了表示熱絡，你可以告訴對方「直接叫我的名字就好了。」例如：你可以告訴對方說「Call me Tom. Everyone does.」（叫我湯姆就行了，大家都這麼叫的。）也可以問對方「我可以直接叫你的名字嗎 ?」例如對方叫做Sally Lin.，你可以問她「Mind if I call you Sally ?」（我叫你莎莉，你會介意嗎？）

有些美國人的名字很長，這些名字常會有簡稱，例如：一般人都叫Elizabeth（伊麗莎白）為Lisa（麗莎），叫Robert（羅勃）為Bob（鮑伯）。若習慣朋友叫你簡稱，在介紹的同時，可以告訴對方自己平常的簡稱，例如：你的全名是Jessica（潔西卡），但你的朋友都叫你Jessie（潔西），你就告訴對方：「Just call me Jessie. Everyone does.」（叫我潔西就行了，大家都這麼叫。）

若對方問你：「Mind if I call you Jessica ?」（我

叫你潔西卡，你會介意嗎？）而你的朋友都是叫你 Jessie，你也希望對方叫你 Jessie，可以告訴對方：「Just plain "Jessie" will do.」（簡單地叫我 Jessie 就可以了。）

✎ 自我介紹

A Hi, my name is Helen.

（嗨，我的名字是海倫。）

B Nice to meet you, Helen, I am Tom.

（海倫，很高興認識你，我叫湯姆。）

✎ 把哥哥介紹給朋友

A Helen, this is my brother, Tom.

（海倫，這是我哥哥湯姆。）

B How do you do ?

（你好。）

C How do you do ?

（你好。）

✎ 把妹妹介紹給朋友

A Mr. Smith, I would like you to meet my sister, Helen.

（史密斯先生，我想要您見見我妹妹海倫。）

B Hello, Helen, I have heard wonderful things about you.

（哈囉，海倫，我常聽人稱讚你。）

✎ 介紹家人

A Good morning, I am Helen.

（早安，我是海倫。）

B Hello, Helen, I am Tom and this is my wife, Judy.

（哈囉，海倫，我是湯姆，這是我太太茱蒂。）

✎ 有人自我介紹你怎麼接腔

A Good afternoon, I am Helen.

（午安，我是海倫。）

B Nice to meet you, Helen.

（海倫，很高興認識你。）

重點單字片語

- ☐ wonderful [ˈwʌndɚfəl] 好棒的
- ☐ member [ˈmɛmbɚ] 會員
- ☐ club [klʌb] 俱樂部
- ☐ past [pæst] 過去的
- ☐ grounds [graʊndz] 場地（ground 的複數）
- ☐ condition [kəˈdɪʃən] 狀況
- ☐ team [tim] 隊伍
- ☐ plain [plen] 平常的
- ☐ as ～ as possible 盡可能的

Sounds good.

（聽起來很好。）

MP3-14

Dialog 1

A If you're not busy tomorrow afternoon, let's play golf.

（如果你明天下午不太忙，我們去打高爾夫球。）

B Tomorrow sounds good.

（明天應該可以。）

What time ?

（什麼時候？）

A How about two o'clock at the club ?

（二點鐘在俱樂部，好嗎？）

B Works for me.

（我沒問題。）

A Good, ask John if he wants to play, too.

（好的，問約翰看看他是不是也想打。）

Dialog 2

A Hey, we are getting together for drinks after work if you want to come.

（嗨，我們下班後要一起去喝酒，如果你想一道來的話。）

B Sounds fun.

（聽起來很有意思。）

Where is everyone going ?

（大家要去哪裡？）

A We are meeting at Chili's around six thirty.

（我們六點半在小辣椒西餐廳見面。）

B Which Chili's ?

（哪一家小辣椒西餐廳？）

A The one just down the street.

（這條街上的那一家。）

B Great, see you there.

（好，那裡見。）

Dialog 3

A Sunday night I am having a cocktail party.

（星期日晚上我會開一個雞尾酒會。）

You should come by.

（你應該來。）

B What's the occasion ?

（那是什麼樣的宴會？）

A My husband just got a promotion at work.

（我先生在公司剛剛得到升遷。）

B That's great !

（那真棒！）

A Do you think you can make it ?

（你想你能來嗎？）

B Sure, see you there.

（當然可以，我們在那兒見。）

你一定要知道

老外說英語時，不會一字一句規規矩矩的說，有時會把主詞省略掉，但是省略掉的主詞若是第三人稱單數，其動詞仍然必須加個「s」。例如：常見的「Sounds great.」（很好）、「Sounds fine to me.」（我認為很好）和「Works for me.」（我沒問題）都是省略掉主詞「That」。

以上提到的常見口語：「Sounds great.」（很好）、「Sounds fine to me.」（我認為很好）、「Sounds like a good idea.」（是個好主意）和「Works for me.」（我沒問題）等，都是用在對方提出的意見，你認為很好時所回答的句子。

✎ 在家辦酒會

A Are you free Sunday night for a cocktail party at my house ?

（星期日晚上，你有空來參加我們家的雞尾酒會嗎？）

B Sorry, but I have other plans.

（對不起，但我已經有其他的計劃。）

✎ 邀人打高爾夫球

A Would you like to play golf tomorrow afternoon ?

（你明天下午要打高爾夫球嗎？）

B Yes, how about two o'clock at the club ?

（好的，二點鐘在俱樂部，怎麼樣？）

✎ 邀人參加宴會

A I am having a party Saturday night.

（星期六晚上，我要開一個宴會。）

Stop by if you want.

（如果你想要來的話就過來。）

B I would love too, but I already have plans.

（我很想過來，但我已經有其他的計劃。）

✎ 約朋友到餐廳

A If you're free after work, stop by Chili's.

（如果你下班後有空，到小辣椒西餐廳來。）

B Sounds great.

（聽起來是一個好主意。）

I will see you there.

（我們在那裡見。）

重點單字片語

- ☐ cocktail [ˈkɑkˌtel] 雞尾酒
- ☐ promotion [prəˈmoʃən] 升官
- ☐ occasion [əˈkeʒən] 場合；原因
- ☐ get together 聚在一起
- ☐ after work 下班後
- ☐ come by 過來
- ☐ stop by 過來一下

What time and where ?
（幾點，在哪裡？）

MP3-15

Dialog 1

A I need a photographer for my wedding.

（我的婚禮上需要一個攝影師。）

And I'd like to see your portfolio.

（我想要看看您的作品集。）

B I can meet with you any time next week.

（下個禮拜任何時候，我都可以跟你見面。）

A Next Wednesday is good for me.

（下個禮拜三我有時間。）

B Sounds fine.

（很好。）

What time and where ?

（幾點，在哪裡？）

A Let's meet at the Hilton around two o'clock.

（兩點鐘在希爾頓飯店見面。）

B See you there.

（到時候見。）

I will call if I need to reschedule.

（如果我必須另訂時間的話，會打電話給你。）

Dialog 2

A I need to talk to you about this proposal.

（我必須跟你談談這個企畫。）

B OK, how does dinner sound ?

（好的，晚飯時間怎麼樣？）

A Sounds fine to me.

（我沒問題。）

Where would you like to meet ?

（你想要在哪裡見面？）

B Meet me at the café on the corner.

（在街角的那家小餐館見我。）

A I will see you there at seven.

（七點鐘，我在那裡跟你見面。）

B OK.

（好的。）

Dialog 3

A We need to get together and discuss this contract.

（我們必須聚在一起，討論這個合約。）

B OK, can you be at my office around two today ?

（好的，今天大約兩點，你可以到我的辦公室來嗎？）

A Two is not good for me.

（兩點我不方便。）

How about ten o'clock tomorrow morning ?

（明天早上十點，怎麼樣？）

B That sounds fine.

（好的。）

A O.K. I will see you then.

（好，到時候再見。）

你一定要知道

在商議一件事情時，你若是要提出建議，可以用 How about 後面接所提議的意見，來徵詢大家的意見。例如：大家在商議見面的時間，你提出星期五，就可以問：「How about Friday ?」

談到時間，有個字在英語會話中經常會用到，它就是 anytime。它是指「任何時間都可以」。例如：有人要跟你約定時間，你認為下個星期隨時都沒問題，說法就是：「Anytime next week is good for me.」

一般來說，你要找人設計或製作東西，會要求看對方的作品，來判斷他是否能勝任你要求的工作，整句話的說法就是：「I'd like to see your portfolio.」

✎ 邀約見面

A I need to see you to discuss this contract.

（我需要見你，討論這個合約。）

B Meet me tomorrow morning at nine in my office.

（明天早上九點鐘，到我的辦公室見我。）

✎ 約時間見面

A Let's have lunch tomorrow and discuss this new policy.

（明天我們一起吃午飯，討論這個新政策。）

B Tomorrow is not good for me.

（明天我不方便。）

How about Friday？

（星期五怎麼樣？）

✎ 想看作品集

A When can I set up an appointment to see your portfolio ?

（我什麼時間，可以來看你的作品集？）

B Anytime next week is good for me.

（下禮拜，任何時候都沒有問題。）

✎ 商量見面時間

A When can we get together to discuss this memo ?

（我們什麼時候可以一起討論一下這個公文？）

B Give me twenty minutes.

（給我二十分鐘。）

And I will meet you in the conference room.

（然後我們在會議室見面。）

✎ 約定見面

A Can we meet over lunch to discuss this proposal ?

（我們可以在午餐見面時，討論這個企畫案嗎？）

B Yes, let's meet at the cafe down the street.

（好的，讓我們在街上那間小餐館見面。）

重點單字片語

- ☐ contract [ˈkɑntrækt] 合約
- ☐ policy [ˈpɑləsɪ] 政策
- ☐ portfolio [portˈfolɪˌo] 作品選集
- ☐ memo [ˈmɛmo] 公文；備忘錄（memorandum 簡寫）
- ☐ conference [ˈkɑnfərəns] 會議
- ☐ conference room 會議室
- ☐ discuss [dɪˈskʌs] 討論
- ☐ proposal [prəˈpozl̩] 企畫
- ☐ café [kəˈfe] 小餐館；咖啡館
- ☐ photographer [fəˈtɑgrəfɚ] 攝影師
- ☐ wedding [ˈwɛdɪŋ] 結婚；婚禮
- ☐ corner [ˈkɔrnɚ] 角落
- ☐ set up 設定

Please keep in touch.

（要聯絡哦！）

MP3-16

Dialog 1

A Tom, it was nice seeing you again.

（湯姆，很高興再見到你。）

B Same here, tell your family hello.

（我也是，替我向你的家人問好。）

A I will.

（我會的。）

And we will have to get together again sometime.

（我們有空該聚一聚。）

B I know.

（我知道。）

Give me a call and we can set up a dinner date.

（打電話給我，我們可以一起吃晚餐。）

A Sounds like a good idea.

（聽起來是個好主意。）

Take care.

（保重。）

Dialog 2

A It was a pleasure seeing you again.

（很高興再見到你。）

B Same here.

（我也是。）

You look great.

（你看起來很好。）

A Thanks. Please tell Robert I said hello.

（謝謝你，請告訴羅勃我向他問好。）

B Sure, and tell the kids I said hello as well.

（好的，告訴你的孩子，我也向他們問好。）

A Take care and please stay in touch.

（保重，要聯絡哦！）

B I will.

（我會的。）

Drive safely.

（開車小心。）

Dialog 3

A I would like to thank you for coming by today.

（謝謝您今天過來。）

B No problem, I am always interested in any new policy changes.

（沒什麼，我對任何新的政策改變都很有興趣。）

A Well, I hope you were pleased with the results of the meeting.

（那麼，我希望你對會議的結果還滿意。）

B Very pleased, I must say.

（我必須承認，我很滿意。）

A It was good to see you again.

（很高興再見到您。）

Call if you have any questions.

（如果有任何問題，打電話給我。）

B I will, thanks.

（我會的，謝謝。）

你一定要知道

聚會結束，跟朋友道別時，若你與對方是在那一次的聚會中才剛認識，要先說「很高興認識你」，像「Good to meet you.」或「It was a pleasure meeting you.」或「It was nice meeting you.」說完這句話，再說道別的話，如：「Have a nice evening.」（晚安）、「Good night.」（晚安）、「Good-bye.」（再見）等。

在一個聚會結束，大家互相道別時，若你與對方是本來就認識，說再見之前要說「很高興再見到你」，例如「Good to see you again.」或「It was a pleasure seeing you again.」或「It was nice seeing you again.」至於道別的話，除了以上提到的，還可以用「Take care.」（保重）、「Please keep in touch.」（要保持聯繫）、「Bye. Take it easy.」（再見，要保重）、「So long.」（再見）、「See you later.」（再見）、「Talk to you later.」（以後再聊）等等。

聚會結束，跟朋友道別時，如果有人跟你說：「It was a pleasure seeing you again.」，你可以回答「Same here.」（我也是。）表示「我也很高興再見到你。」

與朋互相道別時，你通常要跟主人說：「Thanks for inviting me.」（謝謝你邀請我），而主人通常會跟客人說：「Thanks for coming.」（謝謝你來）或「Thanks for stopping by.」，再說道別的話。

sometime 這個字是說未來的某個時間，例如你跟朋友說，我們找個時間一起吃飯（have dinner together），整句話就是：「Let's have dinner together sometime.」或是說，我有空會過來坐坐（stop by），也是沒指明何時，說法就是「I'll stop by sometime.」

✎ 道別

A Good to see you again.

（很高興再見到你。）

B Nice to see you, too.

（我也很高興再見到你。）

Drive safely.

（開車小心。）

✎ 互相道別

A It was a pleasure seeing you again.

（很高興再見到你。）

B Please keep in touch.

（要保持聯絡。）

✎ 作客結束

A Thanks for inviting me.

（謝謝您邀請我來。）

B Of course, I hope you enjoyed yourself.

（沒什麼，我希望您玩的愉快。）

✎ 會議結束

A Thanks for stopping by the meeting.

（謝謝您來參加會議。）

B No problem, I think things went well.

（沒什麼，我覺得事情進行得很好。）

✎ 宴會結束

A Have a nice night and tell everyone hello for me.

（晚安，替我向大家問個好。）

B Thanks, the party was beautiful.

（謝謝您，這個宴會很棒。）

重點單字片語

☐ touch [tʌtʃ]	聯絡
☐ drive [draɪv]	開車
☐ safely [ˈseflɪ]	平安地
☐ pleasure [ˈplɛʒɚ]	愉快的事
☐ inviting [ɪnˈvaɪtɪŋ]	邀請（invite 的動名詞）
☐ enjoy [ɪnˈdʒɔɪ]	喜歡；享樂
☐ date [det]	約會
☐ problem [ˈprɑbləm]	問題
☐ changes [ˈtʃendʒɪz]	改變（change 的複數）
☐ results [rɪˈzʌlts]	結果（result 的複數）
☐ thanks for ～	為～謝謝
☐ enjoy yourself	玩得很愉快
☐ stop by	到某處短暫停留
☐ keep in touch	保持聯繫
☐ get together	聚在一起
☐ take care	保重
☐ set up	設定
☐ come by	過來拜訪

Chapter 5 寒暄打招呼

Do you think it will rain ?
(你認為會下雨嗎？)

MP3-17

Dialog 1

A Can you believe how hot it is ?

(你相信竟然有這麼熱的天氣嗎？)

B No ! I wonder when this heat wave will end.

(真不敢相信，不知道這股熱浪什麼時候會結束。)

A The weather report said that we might have rain tonight.

(氣象報告說今晚可能會下雨。)

B Really ? I was hoping it would rain.

（真的嗎？我一直希望會下雨。）

A Me too.

（我也是。）

It will be a nice break from the heat.

（下雨應該會讓天氣不這麼熱。）

Dialog 2

A Oh ! Did it just start raining ?

（噢！剛剛開始下雨了嗎？）

B Yeah, it's pouring.

（是啊，傾盆大雨。）

It just started as I was getting out of the car.

（我走出車子後，才開始下的。）

A I didn't bring the umbrella.

（而且我沒帶雨傘。）

I'm afraid I'll get stuck here for a while.

（所以恐怕我要被困在這一陣子了。）

B Are you in a hurry to go somewhere ?

（你急著要去什麼地方嗎？）

A Not really.

（也沒有。）

Dialog 3

A It sure is humid outside.

（外面真的很潮溼。）

B I know. I can hardly breathe. The air is so thick.

（我知道，我幾乎不能呼吸，空氣這麼悶。）

A Do you think it will rain ?

（你認為會下雨嗎？）

B No, the weather report said the heat wave would not end for two more days.

（不會，氣象報告說這股熱浪兩天後才會結束。）

A Well, I hope he is wrong.

（那麼，我希望他是錯的。）

你一定要知道

不管和誰見面或打招呼，天氣是一個很好的話題，不論天氣好壞，晴天或陰天，都可以當作話題的開端。若有人抱怨天氣，你可以用帶點開玩笑的口吻說「No kidding！」（可不是嗎！）。用 No kidding 是表示你同意對方所說的，只不過是比較俏皮、輕鬆的口氣。如果你要表示對方對天氣的看法，你也注意到了，就說 I know.

若有人預測天氣可能會如何，你雖知道，卻期待情況沒那麼糟時，可用「I'm just hoping that ～」這個句型。

說到天氣，有人喜歡用誇張的語氣說：「你會相信竟然有這樣的天氣嗎？」英語的句型是「Can you believe ～？」，這種句型大都是用在遇到較特殊的情況。天氣狀況總是常有出人意外的時候，因此，常有人會用這個句型打開話題。當有老美以這樣一句話找你搭訕時，你若也覺得實在很熱，你的回答應該是「No」（我也不相信），而不是「Yes」。

✎ 天氣炎熱

A What do you think about this heat ?

（天氣這麼炎熱，你有什麼想法？）

B I have just been hoping it will end !

（我一直希望這炎熱的天氣會過去！）

✎ 預測天氣

A It is cold enough outside to snow.

（外面夠冷了，會下雪的。）

B I know, I am just hoping that it will not freeze.

（我知道，我只希望別被凍壞。）

✎ 談天氣

A According to the weather report, it is supposed to rain tonight.

（根據氣象報告，今晚應該會下雨。）

B I don't think that it will.

（我不認為會下雨。）

✎ 天氣潮濕

A Is the humidity bothering you？

（這種溼度，你不覺得煩嗎？）

B Not really, I am used to it.

（還好啦，我已經習慣了。）

✎ 氣候太潮濕了

A This humidity is terrible！

（這種溼度真令人討厭！）

B No kidding！I feel like I cannot breathe.

（你說的對！我覺得我快不能呼吸了。）

重點單字片語

- ☐ heat [hit] 炎熱
- ☐ end [ɛnd] 結束

- ☐ according [ə'kɔrdɪŋ] 根據
- ☐ weather ['wɛðɚ] 天氣
- ☐ report [rɪ'pɔrt] 報告
- ☐ supposed [sə'pozd] 認為可以（口語）
- ☐ bothering ['bɑðərɪŋ] 困擾（bother 的現在分詞）
- ☐ humidity [hju'mɪdətɪ] 潮濕
- ☐ terrible ['tɛrəbḷ] 令人討厭的（口語）
- ☐ breathe [brið] 呼吸
- ☐ wonder ['wʌndɚ] 想知道
- ☐ break [brek] 短暫的休息
- ☐ humid ['hjumɪd] 潮濕的
- ☐ thick [θɪk] 悶人的
- ☐ pouring ['pɔrɪŋ] 傾倒（pour 的現在分詞）
- ☐ hurry ['hɝɪ] 匆忙
- ☐ wave [wev] 浪潮
- ☐ according to 根據
- ☐ be used to 對～習慣
- ☐ get stuck 困住
- ☐ in a hurry 趕忙
- ☐ heat wave 熱浪

What do you play ?
（你打什麼球？）

MP3-18

Dialog 1

A What kind of sports do you like to watch ?

（你喜歡看哪一種球類？）

B I really don't like any.

（都不喜歡。）

I would rather play.

（我喜歡自己去打。）

A Really ! What do you play ?

（真的！你打什麼球？）

B I play several, but my favorite is golf.

（好幾種，但是我最喜歡的是高爾夫球。）

A I play golf myself.

（我也打高爾夫球。）

We will have to play sometime.

（有空我們應該一起打。）

Dialog 2

A Did you see the baseball game yesterday ?

（你看了昨天的棒球比賽嗎？）

B No. Who played ?

（沒有，哪兩隊在打？）

A The Cubs played the Yankees.

（小熊隊對洋基隊。）

It was an exciting game.

（那一場比賽真刺激。）

B What was so exciting ?

（什麼事那麼刺激？）

A The game was tied and went into the tenth inning.

（比賽打成平手，所以打到第十局。）

Dialog 3

A We are playing in a baseball game this afternoon.

（今天下午我們要打棒球。）

Do you want to play ?

（你要來嗎？）

B No, I am not a very good player.

（不，我打得不好。）

A It doesn't matter.

（沒關係嘛！）

It is just for fun.

（只是好玩而已。）

B Really, I would be uncomfortable.

（真的，我會很尷尬的。）

I would love to watch the game.

（我比較喜歡看。）

A Great！We need fans, too！

（那很好，我們也需要球迷！）

你一定要知道

一群喜歡球類運動的人聚在一起，若前一天有球賽，大家談的話題就是前一天的球賽。用來開始這類話題最平常的句型，就是「Did you see the～game yesterday？」（你昨天看了某一場球賽嗎？），再依前一天是打什麼球，如：baseball、basketball、football、tennis 等等，把該球類放進去句子裡：例如：「Did you see the baseball game yesterday？」（你看了昨天的棒球賽沒？），話題就打開了。

遇到情況較特別時，可以用一種帶點誇張的句型「Can you believe～？」（你會相信有這種事嗎？）來打開話題。

在英語會話中，你常會聽見有人說「Sure thing.」或「Sure did.」這兩句口語。「Sure thing.」是用在答應對方「好的，沒問題」。「Sure did.」用在有人問你有沒有做某件事時，你回答「我做了」時，一般的英語教科書會教你說「Yes, I did.」，這種用法也是正確的；但你若會說「Sure did.」，表示你的英語更溜。

✎ 談球賽

A Did you see the football game yesterday ?

（你有看昨天的足球比賽嗎？）

B Sure did ! Can you believe how long it went ?

（當然看了！你相信比賽竟然會打那麼久嗎？）

✎ 談球賽

A Can you believe the baseball game yesterday ?

（你相信昨天的棒球賽，竟然是那樣嗎？）

B I didn't see the game.

（我沒有看那場比賽。）

What happened ?

（發生了什麼事？）

✎ 邀人打棒球

A Do you want to come and play baseball with us this afternoon ?

（今天下午，你要來跟我們一起打棒球嗎？）

B That would be great !

（那一定很棒。）

What time are you playing ?

（你們什麼時候打？）

✎ 嗜好

A So, do you play any sports ?

（那麼，你有做什麼運動嗎？）

B No, but I golf quite a bit.

（沒有，只是常打高爾夫球。）

✎ 邀友人看球賽

A Do you want to come to my house and watch the game?

（你要到我家來看比賽嗎？）

B No, I have to go to work.

（不，我必須工作。）

I will count on you for the score tomorrow.

（我等你明天告訴我得分。）

重點單字片語

- ☐ **sports** [spɔrts] 運動
- ☐ **occasionally** [əˈkeʒənl̩ɪ] 偶爾的
- ☐ **score** [skor] 得分
- ☐ **exciting** [ɪkˈsaɪtɪŋ] 興奮的
- ☐ **tied** [taɪd] 比數相同（tie 的過去分詞）
- ☐ **inning** [ˈɪnɪŋ] 一局 （棒球）
- ☐ **rather** [ˈræðɚ] 寧可
- ☐ **favorite** [ˈfevərɪt] 最喜歡的

☑ golf [gɔlf] 打高爾夫球

☑ matter [ˈmætɚ] 有關係

☑ uncomfortable [ʌnˈkʌmfɚtəbl̩] 覺得尷尬

☑ fans [fænz] 球迷（fan 的複數）

☑ quite a bit 不少

☑ count on 倚賴

MEMO

What happened ?
（發生了什麼事？）

MP3-19

Dialog 1

A Did you hear about Jane ?

（你聽說珍妮的事了嗎？）

B No. What happened ?

（還沒，發生了什麼事？）

A She won the lottery !

（她中了彩券！）

B Is she going to share ?

（她要跟大家分享嗎？）

A You will have to ask her.

（你必須問問她。）

I haven't been able to find her.

（我一直都找不到她。）

Dialog 2

A Have you seen Tom lately ?

（你最近有看到湯姆嗎？）

B No, I think he has been out of town.

（沒有，我想他出城去了。）

A Too bad. He was great to hang out with.

（太可惜了，跟他在一起很好玩的。）

B Yeah, I know.

（是的，我知道。）

We are supposed to have dinner when he gets back.

（等他回來，我們會一起去吃飯。）

A Well, tell him I said hi and have him call me.

（那，幫我向他問好；並且叫他打電話給我。）

Dialog 3

A Hi, Tom, how have you been ?

（嗨，湯姆，近來好嗎？）

B I've been O.K.

（我很好。）

How about you ?

（你呢？）

A Good.

（很好。）

Where are you going ?

（你要去哪裡？）

B Over to Robert's.

（到羅勃家去。）

How about you ?

（你呢？）

A Oh, I just got off work.

（噢，我剛剛下班。）

你一定要知道

朋友閒聊的時候，偶爾無意中會談起彼此認識的朋友。如果只是問問對方有沒有某人的消息，說法是：「Did you hear about 人？」例如：你想問對方有關 Helen 的消息，就是：「Did you hear about Helen？」若你知道某個朋友最近有不尋常的情況，你問對方是否知道的說法是：「Did You hear that 人遇到某件事？」例如：你知道湯姆到美國去了（went to the United States），你要問對方有沒有聽到這個消息，就是：「Did you hear that Tom went to the United States？」

✎ 聽到謠傳

A Did you hear that Judy won the lottery？

（你聽說茱蒂中了彩券嗎？）

B I heard a rumor, but I didn't believe it.

（我聽到了謠傳，但我不相信。）

✎ 聽到瘋狂的事

A Can you believe what Judy said to the librarian ?

（你會相信茱蒂對圖書館員說的話嗎？）

B No, it was the craziest thing I had ever heard !

（真不敢相信，那是我所聽過最瘋狂的事！）

✎ 問近況

A I wonder where Helen has been lately.

（不知道最近海倫都到哪兒去了？）

B Didn't you hear ?

（你沒有聽說嗎？）

She has gone out of town.

（她出城去了。）

✎ 請人轉告

A If you hear from Mary, tell her to give me a call.

（如果你有看到瑪麗，請她給我打一個電話。）

B I will.

（我會的。）

I want to talk to her, too.

（我也要找她。）

重點單字片語

- ☐ rumor [ˈrumɚ] 謠言
- ☐ librarian [laɪˈbrɛrɪən] 圖書管理員
- ☐ craziest [ˈkrezɪɪst] 最瘋狂的（crazy 的最高級）
- ☐ heard [hɝd] 聽到（hear 的過去式）
- ☐ lately [ˈletlɪ] 近來
- ☐ town [taʊn] 城鎮
- ☐ won [wʌn] 贏，中（win 的過去式）
- ☐ lottery [ˈlɑtərɪ] 彩券

- share [ʃɛr] 共享
- guess [gɛs] 猜想
- each other 互相
- out of town 出城去
- hang out with 在一起

MEMO

I'll be glad to start my vacation.

（很高興快能休假了。）

MP3-20

Dialog 1

A I cannot wait to start my vacation.

（我等不及要休假了。）

B Are you going somewhere ?

（你有打算要去哪裡嗎？）

A Not really, I am just taking a week off from work to relax.

（也沒有，只是想休息一個禮拜，好好放鬆一下。）

B Really, it has been a busy year.

（也是，今年真的很忙。）

Dialog 2

A How was your vacation ?

（你的假期過得怎樣？）

B It was wonderful !

（非常好！）

I will have to show you the pictures.

（我會讓你看照片。）

A What did you do ?

（你都做了什麼？）

B A lot of sight-seeing, eating and sleeping !

（到處觀光、吃東西和睡覺！）

A It must have been nice.

（那一定很愉快。）

Dialog 3

A Aren't you about to take off from work ?

（你不是快休假了嗎？）

B Yes. In two days I'm leaving for vacation.

（對啊，再兩天我就休假了。）

A Do you have a trip planned out ?

（你有沒有計畫去旅遊？）

B We are going to the country to stay with family.

（我們打算去鄉下，跟家人待在一起。）

A That should be nice.

（那一定很棒。）

你一定要知道

對上班族來說，休假是最令人期待的一件事，因此同事間一聊起休假，常有談不完的題材。英語中表示假期的單字「vacation」，指的是公司給員工的假期，每個公司的休假政策不同，每個員工的休假日不同，可以休假的日期長短也不一樣。

如果有人問起你的計畫或你正想做的某件事情，你心裡已大致確定，不過因為其它因素，還不能很肯定時，可以用 hopefully 來回答對方，表示目前為止你並不肯定。例如有人問你，你何時要休假，你雖計畫好在下個星期（next week），但因為工作的關係，你不能很肯定，就說「Hopefully next week.」

另外，有人告訴你一件他覺得很感興奮的事，如果你要表達你完全了解，記住：先說「I can imagine.」這句話總沒錯，接下去就看談的是什麼話題。imagine 是「想像」的意思，「I can imagine.」表示你可以體會對方的心情，對方聽你這麼一說，當然談話的題材就更源源不絕了！

plan out 是表示「把一件事計畫好」的片語。若是問：「是否把行程都計畫好了？」時，由於行程（trip）是被你所計畫的，所以要用過去分詞 planned out，表示被動。這種被動的用法與中文語法不同，要特別注意，英文的說法是：「Do you have a trip planned out？」

✎ 宣佈休假訊息

A I will be glad to start my vacation.

（我很高興快能休假了。）

B I can imagine.

（這我想像得到。）

I would like one myself.

（我自己也想要休假。）

✎ 談休假計畫

A When are you leaving for vacation ?

（你什麼時候要休假？）

B Hopefully the day after next.

（希望是後天。）

I just never know for sure with work.

（我不知道能否把工作搞定。）

✎ 問休假計畫

A What are you going to do on vacation ?

（休假時間，你打算做什麼？）

B Relax and not think about doing anything.

（好好放鬆，什麼事都不做。）

✎ 談旅行計劃

A Are you excited about going to Europe ?

（你要去歐洲了，興奮嗎？）

B Oh, you cannot even imagine !

（噢，你沒辦法想像的！）

I think I might explode !

（我高興得快炸了！）

✎ 假期結束

A When did you get back from your vacation ?

（你什麼時候休假回來的？）

B Last night.

（昨天晚上。）

It was great !

（假期真是棒極了！）

重點單字片語

- ☐ vacation [veˈkeʃən] 假期
- ☐ hopefully [ˈhopfəlɪ] 期待
- ☐ imagine [ɪˈmædʒɪn] 想像
- ☐ relax [rɪˈlæks] 放輕鬆
- ☐ Europe [ˈjʊrəp] 歐洲
- ☐ explode [ɪksˈplod] 爆炸
- ☐ pictures [ˈpɪktʃɚz] 照片（picture 的複數）
- ☐ sight-seeing [ˈsaɪt ˌsiɪŋ] 觀光
- ☐ trip [trɪp] 旅行
- ☐ country [ˈkʌntrɪ] 鄉下
- ☐ plan out 計畫好
- ☐ for sure 確定的
- ☐ take off from work 請假

What's new with your family ?

（家人近來如何？）

MP3-21

Dialog 1

A How has your husband been doing ?

（你先生最近好嗎？）

B Pretty good.

（他很好。）

He has been out of town on business.

（不過他一直在外地出差。）

A Will he be back soon ?

（他會很快回來嗎？）

B Hopefully this weekend.

（我希望這個週末他能回來。）

Dialog 2

A How's the family doing ?

（你的家人都好嗎？）

B O.K. We have all been so busy.

（還好，我們一直都很忙。）

I feel like we never see each other.

（忙得好像好久都沒見面了。）

A I know how you feel.

（我能了解。）

I need more time with mine, too.

（我也希望有更多時間跟家人在一起。）

B I am hoping to take off early Friday and arrange a nice dinner.

（我想星期五早一點下班，安排一頓晚餐。）

A That sounds like a good idea.

（聽起來是一個好主意。）

Dialog 3

A I heard your son got accepted to the National Taiwan University !

（聽說你兒子考上台大了。）

B Yes, he did.

（是啊！）

We are all very proud.

（我們都很為他驕傲。）

A Tell him I said congratulations.

（告訴他，我恭喜他。）

B I will.

（我會。）

I am sure he will appreciate it.

（他一定會很高興的。）

你一定要知道

問候語「What's new ?」本是用在熟悉的朋友間，問對方近來如何，有沒有什麼事情發生。如果要問候的是對方的家人，只需把問候的對象指明，在 What's new 後面先加個 with，再接你要問候的人即可。例如：What's new with your husband ?（你先生最近如何，有沒有什麼事情呢？）

同樣的，我們用來問候對方的英語，如：「How have you been doing ?」或是「How are you doing ?」或是「Is everything good ?」等等，稍加修改都可以用來問候對方的家人。改法就是把主詞換成你要問候的人，例如：你要問對方的先生（husband）好嗎 ?就變成：「How has your husband been doing ?」，「How's your husband doing ?」以及「Is everything good with your husband ?」注意：對方的先生是第三人稱單數，所以 have 要改成 has，are 要改成 is。

若是知道對方的家人正在進行某件事情，如：找工作、找公寓或正要考大學等等，多半會問事情進展得如何，這句的英語句型是：「How is 某件事 going for your 某某人 ?」例如：你朋友的女兒（daughter）在找公寓（the apartment search），英語的說法就是：「How is the apartment search going for your daughter？」

感謝別人的幫忙或謝謝對方的道賀，可以用「Thank you.」或「Thank you very much.」實際上，美國人常愛在 Thank you. 後面加一句「I appreciate it.」（我很感激、高興）。同樣的，有人跟你說，請代我向你的家人說聲恭喜，你也可以回答：「He will appreciate it.」（他會很高興的。）

✎ 問候

A Is everything good with the family？

（你家人都好嗎？）

B Pretty good.

（非常好。）

✎ 誇讚

A It sounds like your son is doing well for himself.

（聽起來你兒子好像做得很出色。）

B Thank you, we are very proud of him.

（謝謝你，我們都很以他為傲。）

✎ 關切

A How is the apartment search going for your daughter？

（你女兒找公寓的事怎麼樣了？）

B I think she found one she liked downtown.

（我想她在市中心，找到她喜歡的了。）

✎ 問學業

A How long until your kids are done with school？

（你的小孩，還有多久才會結束學業？）

B Tom is done this year.

（湯姆是今年。）

And Helen is done in three.

（海倫是三年後。）

✎ 問近況

A What is new with your husband ?

（你先生最近在做什麼？）

B He has been working on building a new deck for the house.

（他在為我們家院子建一個露天平台。）

重點單字片語

- ☑ pretty [ˈprɪtɪ] 相當
- ☑ proud [praʊd] 驕傲的
- ☑ apartment [əˈpɑrtmənt] 公寓
- ☑ search [sɝtʃ] 尋找

- ☐ found [faʊnd] 找到（find 的過去式）
- ☐ building [ˈbɪldɪŋ] 建造（build 的動名詞）
- ☐ deck [dɛk] 露天平台 （庭院）
- ☐ arrange [əˈrendʒ] 安排
- ☐ university [ˌjunəˈvɝsətɪ] 大學
- ☐ accepted [əˈsɛptɪd] 接受（accept 的過去分詞）
- ☐ congratulations [kənˌgrætʃəˈleʃənz] 恭喜
- ☐ appreciate [əˈpriʃɪˌet] 感激
- ☐ are proud of 以～為榮
- ☐ take off 請假；下班

MEMO

Could not be better.

（再好不過了！）

MP3-22

Dialog 1

A How has school been ?

（學校怎麼樣？）

B Could be better.

（不太好。）

I am swamped with homework.

（我快被家庭作業淹死了。）

A I know what you mean.

（我知道你的意思。）

I have a term paper due in two days.

（我有一篇學習報告兩天內要交。）

And I have not started typing.

（而我一個字都還沒寫。）

B No kidding ?

（你不是在開玩笑吧！）

When are you going to do it ?

（你什麼時候要開始做？）

A I am on my way to start now.

（現在正要開始。）

Dialog 2

A What have you been doing in school ?

（你在學校都做什麼？）

B Mostly, I have been caught up in this bridge design project.

（大部份的時間，都在弄這個橋樑設計。）

A Is it a physical model, or a drawing ?

（這次是要做一個具體的模型，還是畫圖就好？）

B It is a physical model.

（要做一個具體的模型。）

We are having a contest.

（我們有一個比賽。）

A Good luck.

（祝好運啦！）

I hope you win.

（希望你會贏。）

Dialog 3

A When do you have to go back to school ?

（你什麼時候要回去上學？）

B A week from tomorrow.

（從明天算起還有一個禮拜。）

A Are you excited ?

（你覺得興奮嗎？）

B Yes and no.

（也是也不是。）

I want to get finished, but I want a longer break also.

（我想把課業結束掉，但也希望能休息久一點。）

你一定要知道

「No kidding.！」是用較輕鬆的語氣表示同意對方的說法。不過它還有另一個用法就是，當對方說的話你不太相信時，也可說「No kidding.！」（你不是在開玩笑吧！）

有人問你的近況，你想回答你的情況很好時，除了「Could not be better.」可以適切表達你的意思以外，還可以炫耀你的英語實力。「Could not be better.」照字面翻譯是「不可能再更好了」，也就是「非常好」的意思。反過來說，情況不太好就是「Could be better.」，照字面翻譯是「還可以更好」。

當對方抱怨遇到困難或不如意的事，為了表示你的關切與瞭解，一句「I know what you mean.」就可以適切地表達了。

簡單會話

✎ 問學校情況

A Is everything going well at school？

（學校一切還好嗎？）

B Could not be better.

（不能再好了。）

I am almost done for the year.

（今年快要結束了。）

✎ 快畢業

A Are you excited about finishing school？

（快畢業了，你覺得興奮嗎？）

B You cannot imagine how excited！

（你沒辦法想像我有多興奮！）

✎ 假期將結束

A Isn't your break just about over ?

（你們的假是不是快要結束了？）

B Yes, classes start in a week.

（是的，學校一個禮拜內就要開課了。）

✎ 上學

A Anything new going on at school ?

（學校裡有什麼事嗎？）

B Not really.

（沒什麼。）

✎ 功課太多

A Can you believe how much studying there is to do for this class ?

（你會相信，這一門課有多少書要念嗎？）

B I know. It seems almost overwhelming.

（我知道，看起來像是應接不暇。）

重點單字片語

- ☐ almost [ɔlˈmost] 幾乎
- ☐ excited [ɪkˈsaɪtɪd] 感到興奮的
- ☐ break [brek] 休息
- ☐ projects [prɑˈdʒɛkts] 研究課題（學校的）
- ☐ overwhelming [ˌovɚˈhwɛlmɪŋ] 壓倒的；應接不暇
- ☐ swamped [swɑmpt] 被淹沒
- ☐ due [dju] 期限截止
- ☐ typing [ˈtaɪpɪŋ] 打字（type 現在分詞）
- ☐ bridge [brɪdʒ] 橋樑
- ☐ design [dɪˈzaɪn] 設計
- ☐ physical [ˈfɪzɪkl] 具體的
- ☐ model [ˈmɑdl̩] 模型
- ☐ drawing [ˈdrɔɪŋ] 繪圖
- ☐ contest [ˈkɑntɛst] 比賽
- ☐ win [wɪn] 贏
- ☐ on my way to 往～的途中
- ☐ go back to school 返回學校上課
- ☐ good luck 祝好運
- ☐ be caught up 被某事纏住

What did you think of Tom's pants ?

（你覺得湯姆的褲子如何？）

MP3-23

Dialog 1

A Do you like this haircut I got ?

（你喜歡我剪的這個髮型嗎？）

B Do you want me to be honest ?

（要我說老實話嗎？）

A Yes, I am really curious.

（是的，我真的很好奇。）

B I think your stylist did a bad job.

（我認為你的髮型師剪得很糟。）

The back is uneven.

（後面剪得參差不齊。）

A I thought so, too.

（我也這麼認為。）

I am going to get a refund.

（我要叫他退錢。）

Dialog 3

A Did you like those pants that Tom had on ?

（你喜歡湯姆穿的褲子嗎？）

B Not really, did you ?

（不怎麼喜歡，你呢？）

A I actually liked the way they looked on him.

（我喜歡湯姆穿那件褲子的樣子。）

I don't know if I would wear them myself.

（但我不確定自己是否會穿。）

B That is as good as saying you don't like them !

（那不就等於你不喜歡！）

A Well...O.K.

（嗯，算是吧！）

Maybe I don't like them.

（或許我不喜歡。）

Dialog 3

A Hey, Helen, that is a great looking sweater !

（嗨，海倫，你這件毛衣很漂亮！）

B Oh, thanks !

（謝謝你！）

I just got it yesterday.

（我昨天剛買的。）

A What do you think of this shirt I got ?

（我買的這件襯衫你覺得怎麼樣？）

B I like it.

（我喜歡。）

你一定要知道

有人讚美你的服裝或身上穿戴的東西時，千萬不要只說「Thank you.」就結束了。可以再接：「I just got it yesterday.」（我昨天買的）、「Do you really like it？」（你真的喜歡？）、「I'm glad you like it.」（很高興你喜歡）、「My wife bought it in Paris.」（我太太在巴黎買的）、「It's a birthday present from my son.」（是我兒子送我的生日禮物）等等。

若服裝的顏色很鮮豔，可以用 bright 形容，口語中也可以用 loud 這個字，像「The tie is too loud.」，就是用來形容領帶顏色很鮮豔，而不是說領帶聲音很大。

若有人問你，對某個人或某個人的衣著看法如何時，你若覺得還可以或不錯，可以用 nice 這個字。例如有人問你昨晚宴會的女主人怎麼樣，你可以說：「She is very nice.」（她人很好。）又有人問你，覺得湯姆穿的鞋子如何時，也可以說：「I thought they are nice.」（我認為他的鞋子很好看。）不過要注意，像鞋子（shoes）、褲子（pants）、眼鏡（glasses）等都是複數，所以要說：「They are nice.」而不是「It is nice.」

✎ 批評別人

A I really think that the shirt Mary wore to the party was horrible.

（我真的認為瑪麗穿去參加宴會的襯衫很糟糕。）

B I have to agree. It was too bright.

（我同意。它太鮮豔了。）

✎ 讚美對方

A I really like that sweater you have on.

（我真的很喜歡你穿的這件毛衣。）

B Thank you. I just got it.

（謝謝，我剛買的。）

✎ 談論穿著

A What did you think of John's pants ?

（你覺得約翰的褲子怎麼樣？）

B I thought they were nice.

（我認為很好。）

But I would not wear them.

（但是我不會穿。）

✎ 問穿著如何

A Did you see what Mary wore to the party last night ?

（你有沒有看到瑪麗昨天穿什麼去參加宴會？）

B No. Was it good or bad ?

（沒有，到底是好還是不好？）

✎ 問髮型如何

A Can I get you to tell me what you think of my haircut ?

（你可以告訴我，你覺得我剪這個髮型怎樣嗎？）

B As long as you don't get mad at me !

（只要你不生氣，我就告訴你。）

重點單字片語

☑ wear [wɛr]	穿；戴
☑ wore [wor]	穿；戴（wear 的過去式）
☑ agree [əˈgri]	同意
☑ horrible [ˈhɔrəbl̩]	（口語）很糟
☑ bright [braɪt]	鮮豔
☑ sweater [ˈswɛtɚ]	毛衣
☑ haircut [ˈhɛrˌkʌt]	剪頭髮
☑ honest [ˈɑnəst]	誠實的
☑ stylist [ˈstaɪlɪst]	髮型師
☑ uneven [ʌnˈivən]	不齊
☑ refund [rɪˈfʌnd]	退款
☑ pants [pænts]	褲子
☑ borrow [ˈbɑro]	借
☑ as good as	等於；同樣
☑ think of	認為
☑ as long as	只要
☑ get mad at	對～生氣

I am glad to be outside.

（我很高興能出來走走。）

MP3-24

Dialog 1

A Can you believe this weather ?

（你相信有這種天氣嗎？）

B I know.

（我知道。）

It is gorgeous.

（天氣真的好棒。）

A I am glad to be outside.

（我很高興能出來走走。）

B Yes, but the bus may be stuffy.

（對啊，但是公車裡的空氣可能會很悶。）

A No, I believe they are air-conditioned.

（不會，我相信公車有空調。）

Dialog 2

A Is this seat taken ?

（這個位子有人坐嗎？）

B No. I'll move over.

（沒有，我挪過去一點。）

A Thanks.

（謝謝您。）

Where are you headed ?

（您要去哪裡？）

B Downtown.

（市中心。）

I have some shopping to do.

（我要買點東西。）

A Me too.

（我也是。）

Dialog 3

A Has the bus for downtown left yet ?

（到市中心的公車開走了嗎？）

B No. I am waiting for the same bus.

（還沒，我也是在等同一班公車。）

A Good. I thought I was late.

（很好，我還以為我遲到了。）

B I think they are behind schedule today.

（我想他們今天有一點誤點。）

A I don't know.

（我也不知道。）

你一定要知道

說到天氣，有人喜歡用誇張的語氣說「你相信竟然有這樣的天氣嗎？」，英語句型是：「Can you believe ～？」例如：「Can you believe how hot it is？」（你相信竟然有這麼熱的天氣嗎？）這種說法不一定在說壞天氣，若遇到長時間的壞天氣，突然天氣轉好了，你也可能聽到有人說：「Can you believe this weather？」

✎ 談天氣

A It is a beautiful day outside！

（今天外面的天氣真好。）

B I know.

（我知道。）

I was just thinking about having lunch outside.

（我正打算到外面吃午餐。）

✎ 詢問座位

A Can I sit down ?

（我可以坐這裡嗎？）

B I'm sorry, I am saving this seat for my friend.

（對不起，這是我為朋友留的位子。）

She just went to get a paper.

（她只是去買個報紙。）

✎ 問開車時間

A The bus hasn't left yet, has it ?

（公車還沒有開走吧？）

B No. I have been here for a few minutes.

（還沒，我來這裡已經好幾分鐘了。）

And I have not seen it.

（還沒見到公車呢！）

✎ 找座位

A Do you mind if I sit down ?

（你介意我坐這個位子嗎？）

B Not at all, there is plenty of room.

（完全不，還有很多空位呢！）

✎ 問票價

A Do you know how much the bus fare is ?

（你知道公車票價是多少嗎？）

B I think it is $10 one way and $20 for an all day pass.

（我想單程是十美元，一整天的乘車券是二十美元。）

重點單字片語

- ☐ saving [ˈsevɪŋ] 保留（save 的現在分詞）
- ☐ fare [fɛr] 車資
- ☐ pass [pæs] 乘車券
- ☐ gorgeous [ˈgɔrdʒəs] 很棒 （口語）

☐ stuffy [ˈstʌfɪ] 很悶

☐ air-conditioned [ˈɛrkən,dɪʃənd] 有冷氣的

☐ downtown [daʊnˈtaʊn] 市中心

☐ schedule [ˈskɛdʒʊl] 時間表

☐ move over 移過去

☐ behind schedule 比預定時間晚

☐ sit down 坐下

☐ how much 多少錢

MEMO

Do you work in the building？
（您在這棟大樓上班嗎？）

MP3-25

Dialog 1

A Hi.

（嗨。）

B Hello. Having a good day？

（哈囉，你今天好嗎？）

A Great！How about yourself？

（很好，你呢？）

B Pretty good.

（非常好。）

We are at mid week.

（這個禮拜已經過去一半了。）

A I know. See you later.

（對啊，再見。）

B Bye.

（再見。）

Dialog 2

A Where are you going ?

（你要去哪裡？）

B Eleven.

（十一樓）

A I'll push the button.

（我來按按鈕。）

B Thanks. Do you work in the building ?

（謝謝，你在這棟大樓上班嗎？）

A Yes, I work on ten. And you ?

（是的，我在十樓，你呢？）

B I am here on business.

（我來這裡出差的。）

Dialog 3

A Have you been having a busy day？

（你今天很忙嗎？）

B Not too bad.

（還好。）

What about you？

（你呢？）

A I can't complain.

（沒什麼可抱怨的。）

B I sure am looking forward to Friday, though.

（但是我還是在等星期五。）

A Me too！

（我也是！）

你一定要知道

同乘一部電梯，有些是相識的，有些是不相識的，隨便閒聊打招呼是常有的事。這類的對話，不外是問對方要到哪一樓、在哪一家公司上班等。

彼此互相問好時，被問候者除了回答對方的問話之外，也要跟對方問候一聲，它的說法包括：「And you？」（你呢？）、「What about you？」（你怎麼樣？）、「How about yourself？」（那你自己呢？）

有人跟你問好，常見的回答有：Great、Not too bad、Fine、Pretty good. 等等。另外有兩個口語也常用，如果你覺得剛剛那幾個太通俗了，以下這兩個口語就相當好用：「I can't complain.」（沒什麼可抱怨的。）和「Couldn't be better.」（不可能再更好。）complain 是「抱怨」的意思，若沒什麼可抱怨的，就是說日子過得很好。

在口語中，疑問句不一定就是一板一眼的疑問句形式，例如要問「我們要去吃飯，你要不要一起來？」，美國人會說：「You want to come along？」而不是：「Do you want to come along？」不會加上 Do，但句尾語調會提高。

美國一個星期上班五天，所以大家都在等星期五的到來，又可以再休息兩天。常見的說法是：「I can't wait for Friday to get here！」或「I am looking forward to Friday.」

✎ 搭電梯

A What floor？

（到幾樓？）

B Ten, please.

（到十樓。）

✎ 打招呼

A Been busy today？

（今天很忙嗎？）

B A little, but not nearly as much as yesterday！

（有一點，但不像昨天那麼忙！）

✎ 問候

A How has your day been ?

（今天好嗎？）

B Good. I am finally catching up with all my work.

（很好，我終於趕上我所有的工作了。）

✎ 寒暄

A Where are you going for lunch ?

（你要去哪裡吃午飯？）

B We are going to KFC.

（我們要去肯德基炸雞店。）

You want to come along ?

（你要一起來嗎？）

✎ 閒聊

A I can't wait for Friday to get here !

（我等不及到星期五！）

B Really. I am pretty worn out.

（是真的，我累壞了。）

重點單字片語

- ☐ floor [flor] 層（樓房的）
- ☐ nearly ['nɪrlɪ] 幾乎
- ☐ mid [mɪd] 中間
- ☐ push [pʊʃ] 按
- ☐ button ['bʌtn̩] 按鈕
- ☐ seventeen [ˌsɛvən'tin] 十七
- ☐ complain [kəm'plen] 抱怨
- ☐ forward ['fɔrwɚd] 向前
- ☐ be worn out 累壞了
- ☐ catch up with 趕上
- ☐ come along 一起來
- ☐ look forward to 期待

My child is sick.
（我的小孩病了。）

MP3-26

Dialog 1

A What an adorable child !

（這個小孩子好可愛！）

B Thanks. He is a little sick right now.

（謝謝您，不過他現在生病。）

A Oh. Do you not have a pediatrician ?

（哦，你們沒有小兒科醫生嗎？）

B We do, but he had no appointment available.

（我們有的，但是他都沒有空。）

A I see.

（原來如此。）

Dialog 2

A Have you seen this doctor before ?

（你以前看過這個醫生嗎。）

B Yes, he is our regular doctor. Why ?

（是的，他是我們固定的醫生。為什麼這麼問？）

A I have never seen him before.

（我以前沒有看過他。）

And I wonder if he is good.

（我在想不曉得他好不好。）

B I came from another doctor's office to him.

（我是從其他醫生那裡轉到這裡來的。）

He is very good.

（他非常棒。）

A Good. That makes me feel a lot better.

（很好，你說的話讓我覺得好多了。）

Dialog 3

A Is the doctor running on schedule ?

（醫生會按照約定時間看診嗎？）

B No. He had an emergency.

（不，他有個急診。）

A How long is the wait now ?

（那現在要等多久？）

B About thirty minutes.

（大約三十分鐘。）

A Wow ! Maybe I should reschedule.

（哇！或許我應該另外再約時間。）

B I think I might as well.

（我也想另外約個時間。）

你一定要知道

在醫院裡寒暄的內容，多為「How long is the wait now？」（還要等多久？）、「My child is sick.」（我的小孩病了）、「Have you seen this doctor before？」（你以前看過這個醫生嗎？）、「Is this your regular doctor？」（你固定看這個醫生嗎？）等等這一類的對話。熟記本課句型對話，到時就可以清楚表達自己的意思了。

✎ 小孩生病

A Your child is very cute！

（你的小孩很可愛！）

B Thank you very much.

（非常謝謝您。）

She is not feeling well today, though.

（但是他今天不太舒服。）

✎ 久等醫師

A Why is the doctor not on time？

（醫生為什麼不準時？）

B He had to go to the hospital for an emergency.

（因為有緊急的事件，他要到醫院去。）

✎ 在醫院裡

A I am always nervous at the doctor's office.

（在醫生診所，我總是很緊張。）

B Don't worry. I am, too.

（別擔心，我也是。）

✎ 看醫生

A Is this your regular doctor？

（這是您固定看的醫生嗎？）

B Yes. We have gone to her for six years.

（是的，我們讓她看診，已經有六年了。）

✎ 談論醫生

A I hope this doctor is good with children.

（我希望這個醫生擅長看小孩子。）

B Oh, don't worry.

（哦，別擔心。）

He is the best.

（他是最好的。）

重點單字片語

- ☐ hospital [ˈhɑspɪtl̩] 醫院
- ☐ emergency [ɪˈmɝdʒənsɪ] 緊急事件
- ☐ nervous [ˈnɝvəs] 緊張的
- ☐ worry [ˈwɝɪ] 擔心
- ☐ regular [ˈrɛgjələ˞] 一般的
- ☐ adorable [əˈdorəbl̩] 可愛的
- ☐ pediatrician [ˌpidɪəˈtrɪʃən] 小兒科醫生
- ☐ available [əˈveləbl̩] 有空的

☐	appointment [ə'pɔɪntmənt]	約定時間
☐	schedule ['skɛdʒʊl]	時間表
☐	reschedule [rɪ'skɛdʒʊl]	重新約定時間
☐	on schedule	按照預定時間
☐	on time	準時

MEMO

Don't worry about it.
（沒關係。）

MP3-27

Dialog 1

A Oops, I'm sorry.

（唉呀！對不起。）

I did not mean to bump into you.

（我不是故意撞上你的。）

B Don't worry about it.

（沒關係。）

A I was watching that bird instead of the trail !

（我在看著那一隻鳥而沒有在看路！）

B Where is the bird ?

（鳥在哪裡？）

A Right over there, above the red sign.

（就在那兒，紅色招牌上面。）

B Oh, I see it, too.

（哦，我也看到了。）

Dialog 2

A Do you know where the restroom is ?

（你知道洗手間在哪裡嗎？）

B Yes, it is just on the other side of that fence.

（知道，就在籬笆的另外一邊。）

A I'm sorry, where ?

（對不起，在哪裡？）

B Just take the trail to the left and you can't miss it.

（你就沿著這條路走，左轉，不會找不到的。）

A Thanks !

（謝謝您！）

Dialog 3

A The park sure is quiet today.

（今天公園真的很安靜。）

B I know. Everyone is at the parade.

（我知道，每一個人都去看遊行了。）

A There is a parade today ?

（今天有遊行嗎？）

B Oh. Yes, over on First street.

（哦，是的，在第一街。）

A I'm glad that I pay attention !

（我很高興注意到了！）

B I'll be going over there later if you want to go with me.

（我稍後會過去那裡，如果你想跟我一起去。）

你一定要知道

老外都很熱情，不管你是在休閒場所或在公園裡，碰到不認識的人可能都會聊上幾句。所以只要看到老外，就是練習英語會話最好的機會。

有人不小心撞上了你，或是做什麼冒犯了自己，向你道歉時，你可以說「Don't worry about that.」表示「沒關係」，請對方別耿耿於懷。

✎ 詢問活動

A I never know when these things are happening.

（我都不曉得這些活動何時要舉行。）

B They really did not advertise it this year.

（今年他們的確不太做廣告。）

✎ 在公園

A I wonder where everyone is.

（我懷疑大家都到哪裡去了？）

B I think there is a parade downtown.

（我聽說市中心有一個遊行。）

✎ 找飲水機

A Excuse me, where is the drinking fountain ?

（對不起，飲水機在哪裡？）

B I don't know.

（我不知道。）

I am not from around here.

（我不住在這附近。）

✎ 撞到別人

A Oh, did I hit you ?

（我撞上你了嗎？）

B Well, we may have hit each other.

（嗯，我們可能互相撞上對方了。）

I was lost in thought.

（我在想別的事情。）

✎ 找帽子

A Did you see a red hat on this bench when you sat down ?

（你坐下的時候，有沒有看到一頂紅帽子在這張長椅子上。）

B No, I am sorry.

（沒有，很對不起。）

You might check with the lost and found later in the week.

（一個星期後，你可以到失物招領中心問問看。）

重點單字片語

☑ advertise [ˈædvɚˌtaɪz] 廣告

☑ parade [pəˈred] 遊行

☑ fountain [ˈfaʊntn̩]	噴水池
☑ drinking fountain	飲水機
☑ hit [hɪt]	撞到
☑ lost [lɔst]	迷失
☑ bench [bɛntʃ]	長凳子
☑ trail [trel]	路徑
☑ sign [saɪn]	招牌
☑ rest room	洗手間
☑ fence [fɛns]	籬笆
☑ miss [mɪs]	錯過
☑ attention [əˈtɛnʃən]	注意力
☑ lost in thought	想著別的事情
☑ lost and found	失物招領處
☑ instead of	而不是
☑ pay attention	注意
☑ bump into	撞上～

This is a great party !

（這個宴會真成功！）

MP3-28

Dialog 1

A This is a great party !

（這個宴會真成功！）

B It is.

（沒錯。）

I was a little worried because it was on a weeknight.

（我原先有點擔心，因為不是在週末晚上。）

A I think everyone needed a break from reality !

（我想每個人都需要在現實生活中休閒一下！）

B I know I do.

（我知道我自己是需要的。）

A Me too !

（我也是！）

I am going for a drink.

（我要去拿杯飲料。）

B See you later.

（待會見。）

Dialog 2

A I am going to the bar.

（我要到吧檯。）

Would you like me to get you a drink ?

（要我幫你拿個飲料嗎？）

B No. I am fine.

（不用，我不渴。）

A Are you sure ?

（你確定嗎？）

I don't mind.

（我不介意幫你拿的。）

B O.K., could you please get me a whisky ?

（好的，可否請你幫我拿杯威士忌？）

A Absolutely ! I'll be right back.

（沒問題！我馬上回來。）

Dialog 3

A Hi. Did you just get here ?

（嗨，你剛到嗎？）

B Yes. I got tied up in traffic.

（是的，我被塞在路上。）

A It is bad coming into downtown.

（市中心的交通實在很槽。）

B Really ! Have a lot of people shown up ?

（沒錯。已經有很多人來了嗎？）

A Quite a few.

（不少人。）

More should be coming later.

（待會應該會有更多人。）

你一定要知道

一群人在酒會中聊天，如果想去拿飲料，可以順便問一下對方，要不要順道幫他拿一杯，英文的說法是：「Would you like me to get you a drink？」（要我幫你拿個飲料嗎？）或「Can I get you anything？」（你要我幫你拿點什麼嗎？）。有人這麼問你時，若不想麻煩對方，就說「No, I am fine.」（不用了，我不渴。）

有人請你幫他做件事，你願意做，可以回答「Absolutely！」這個字比 O.K. 或 Yes（好的）語氣更強。若有人問你要不要某樣東西，你要，也是可以回答「Absolutely！」例如你到朋友家作客，朋友問你：「Do you want another piece of cake？」（你還要再吃一塊蛋糕嗎？），若還想要，就可以回答「Absolutely！」

✎ 找路

A Did you get here okay？

（我們這裡好找嗎？）

B No. The directions were pretty bad.

（不好找，方向指示非常不清楚。）

✎ 宴會盛況

A Are there a lot of people coming tonight ?

（今天晚上會有很多人來嗎？）

B Not too many - about fifty.

（不太多，大約有五十個。）

✎ 稱讚

A I can't believe how great this place looks.

（我真不相信這個地方這麼棒。）

B I think they spent about two days getting ready !

（聽說他們花了兩天的時間準備！）

✎ 拿飲料

A Excuse me. I am going to the bar for another drink.

（對不起，我要去吧檯再拿一杯飲料。）

B Would you mind getting me a whisky while you are up ?

（你過去的時候，介意幫我拿杯威士忌嗎？）

✎ 喝飲料

A Can I get you anything while I am at the bar ?

（我過去吧檯的時候，要我幫你拿什麼飲料嗎？）

B No thanks. I just got a full drink.

（不用了，謝謝，我剛剛喝了很多。）

重點單字片語

- ☐ directions [dəˈrɛkʃənz] 方向指示
- ☐ bar [bɑr] 吧檯
- ☐ whisky [ˈhwɪskɪ] 威士忌酒
- ☐ absolutely [ˈæbsəˌlutlɪ] 好的、沒問題（口語）
- ☐ reality [rɪˈælɪtɪ] 現實
- ☐ break [brek] 短暫的休息
- ☐ traffic [ˈtræfɪk] 交通
- ☐ got tied up 被困住
- ☐ show up 出現
- ☐ quite a few 好幾個

國家圖書館出版品預行編目資料

5分鐘征服英語會話/張瑪麗, Scott William合著. -- 新北市：哈福企業有限公司, 2022.11
面；　公分. -- (英語系列；81)
ISBN 978-626-96215-9-0(平裝)
1.CST: 英語 2.CST: 會話
805.188　　111017292

5分鐘征服英語會話（附QR Code行動學習音檔）

作者／張瑪麗・Scott William — 合著
責任編輯／Lilibet Chang
封面設計／李秀英
內文排版／Lin Lin House
出版者／哈福企業有限公司
地址／新北市板橋區五權街16 號 1 樓
電話／(02) 2808-4587
傳真／(02) 2808-6545
郵政劃撥／31598840
戶名／哈福企業有限公司
出版日期／2022 年 11 月
定價／NT$ 369 元
港幣定價／123 元
封面內文圖/ 取材自Shutterstock

全球華文國際市場總代理／采舍國際有限公司
地址／新北市中和區中山路2段366巷10號3樓
電話／(02) 8245-8786
傳真／(02) 8245-8718
網址／www.silkbook.com 新絲路華文網

香港澳門總經銷／和平圖書有限公司
地址／香港柴灣嘉業街12 號百樂門大廈17 樓
電話／(852) 2804-6687
傳真／(852) 2804-6409

email ／ welike8686@Gmail.com
facebook ／ Haa-net 哈福網路商城

電子書格式：PDF

哈福

哈福